***"I scare you, don't I?"* Philip asked.**

"I can't help it. I wasn't born with much of a backbone. Congenital defect. Go ahead, though— I'm braced. What do we have ahead of us?" Jennifer asked.

His eyes had become very bright. "A long night."

"And?" she said with acute apprehension.

"I'd like you to spend it with me," he said gently.

With a low moan, she slid downward in her seat, pulling her brown tweed hat down to cover her entire face. She heard his laughter as the car moved into reverse, then traveled down Lake Drive. His hand came to her shoulder and rubbed lightly.

"It doesn't matter," he said in a kind tone. "There are other ways to do these things. For example, we could date, if you think that would be reassuring."

Jennifer thought, I'm dreaming all this. Her voice, muffled by the hat, said, "Date?"

"Date. That phenomenon of human behavior where you devote a goodly amount of time to wondering what to wear, and I empty the old McDonald's cartons out of the car, and we both take showers and wear clean underwear just in case—I beg your pardon?"

"Nothing." Muffled voice. "I moaned."

"You do that a lot."

"Only around you."

"That's a promising sign . . . ."

WHAT ARE *LOVESWEPT* ROMANCES?

They are stories of true romance and touching emotion. We believe those two very important ingredients are constants in our highly sensual and very believable stories in the *LOVESWEPT* line. Our goal is to give you, the reader, stories of consistently high quality that may sometimes make you laugh, sometimes make you cry, but are always fresh and creative and contain many delightful surprises within their pages.

Most romance fans read an enormous number of books. Those they truly love, they keep. Others may be traded with friends and soon forgotten. We hope that each *LOVESWEPT* romance will be a treasure—a "keeper." We will always try to publish

LOVE STORIES YOU'LL NEVER FORGET
BY AUTHORS YOU'LL ALWAYS REMEMBER

The Editors

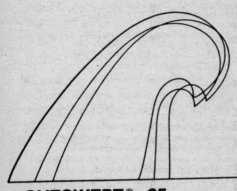

LOVESWEPT® • 25

Sharon & Tom Curtis
Lightning That Lingers

 BANTAM BOOKS • NEW YORK • TORONTO • LONDON • SYDNEY

LIGHTNING THAT LINGERS

A Bantam Book / December 1983
Silver Signature edition / July 1991

LOVESWEPT® *and the wave device are registered trademarks of Bantam Books, a division of Bantam Doubleday Dell Publishing Group, Inc. Registered in U.S. Patent and Trademark Office and elsewhere.*

If you would be interested in receiving protective vinyl covers for your Loveswept books, please write to this address for information:

Loveswept
Bantam Books
P.O. Box 985
Hicksville, NY 11802

ISBN 0-553-21630-9

Published simultaneously in the United States and Canada

Bantam Books are published by Bantam Books, a division of Bantam Doubleday Dell Publishing Group, Inc. Its trademark, consisting of the words "Bantam Books" and the portrayal of a rooster, is Registered in U.S. Patent and Trademark Office and in other countries. Marca Registrada. Bantam Books, 666 Fifth Avenue, New York, New York 10103.

PRINTED IN THE UNITED STATES OF AMERICA

O   0 9 8 7 6 5 4 3

Our heartfelt thanks to Edith and Jane (for daring research), and to Nancy Frank, Lois and Elmer, Dr. Ed Eloranta, Georgia Walden, Ceci Chappel, and Maureen and Robert who helped us explore the hidden reaches of the Pabst Mansion. And special thanks to Earl the Owl.

This book is dedicated to George and Kathleen Blakslee, with much love.

One

The night wind drove needle-like snow into the young man's back as he kicked the heavy door closed behind him. There was no heat in the huge main hall of the mansion, and his footsteps echoed in the open emptiness as he stamped sticky snowflakes from his boots and shook them from his shoulders. Country darkness had fallen outside hours ago, and only a thin slip of muted moonlight poured like liquid silver seafoam down the grand staircase from the tall windows on the first landing.

But there was no hesitancy in the man's stride as he walked through the shadowed quiet of the hall. He had crossed this floor uncounted times since he had taken his first faltering steps here twenty-seven years ago, when his mother had released his baby fingers and watched in laughing excitement as he toddled into his father's outstretched arms. Gone was that laughing mother with the gentle hands and the whispered fragrance of gardenia. Gone was the father with the moustache that made his kisses tickle.

Walking in the cavernous gloom, alone except for the tiny burden under his pullover that he supported with both hands, the man felt no unease. His nature was at times a whimsical one, but even as a child he had never been fearful. And he was not completely devoid of company.

"I'm home, Chaucer," he called softly in the darkness. Hampered by the limitations of human hearing, he missed the owl's silent flight, though he could feel the slight draft from its wings brush his wind-stung skin, and the light weight of padded feet coming to rest expertly on his shoulder with a subtle shift in balance. There was a musical trill of greeting. The man resettled the burden under his pullover and withdrew one hand, dragging off a suede glove with his teeth. He reached up and gently scratched the owl's silky breast with a friendly finger.

"We have company, old son," he said, the very attractive voice husky from the heavy cold outdoors. "Orphans. Orphans of the storm. How are your parental instincts functioning?"

A wing, lifted indignantly, touched the back of his head as the owl hissed, and that drew a slight laugh from the man.

Together they passed under the high cool ceilings, going by the small dry fountain and ceramic pool. In the vast dining room, a huge chandelier dense with dusty prisms sparkled above them in the dimness, and answered the man's footsteps with a faint chime. Beyond, he passed the summer dining room and the butler's pantry. At last he came gratefully into the kitchen, where the antiquated central heating had been puffing a steady, pillowy warmth. His hand hit the upper button of the old-fashioned light switch, flooding the warm wide expanse of the room with cheerful yellow light, and his eyes, night-adjusted, stung. He registered the fact briefly, instinctively, by its biology: the rapid decomposition of rhodopsin in the eye.

Crossing the parquet floor, he knelt by a low cupboard, withdrawing a cardboard shoe box. Working one-handed, he lined the box with a clean dishtowel, and then set it on the rosewood work table. With utmost care, he reached under his pullover and brought out his two tiny orphans, supporting them carefully in his cupped hands. He brought them level with his face and looked at them closely.

"Well," he said softly. "Welcome to my nest."

The two little owlets blinking sleepily at him from his palms were balls of gray down, all beak and brilliant lemon-yellow eyes that were beginning to focus on him with alert annoyance at having been roused from their sleeping place next to his warm, dry skin and his soothing heartbeat. They seemed suddenly to remember that they were hungry and began to chatter loudly.

The adult screech owl on the man's shoulder shot off like a catapulted weight and swept up to perch on the high cupboard, hunching his wings and watching the noisy duo with evident disgust, clacking his beak before turning his head pointedly away.

"What's the matter, you old bachelor?" the man asked with amusement. "Aren't you cut out for fatherhood? Anyone would think I haven't told you time and again that birds of a feather flock together." The screech owl raised his ear-tufts and turned his head back enough to give the man a sardonic half-lidded look. Smiling back, the man said, "So. Let's get on with seeing what we can do about ensuring the survival of the species."

He deposited the owlets gently in the box before shrugging out of his jacket. They kept him busy for the next hour, their voices rising in penetrating squeals while he chopped raw beef for them, keeping it in the oven just long enough to take off the chill, then mixing it with the downy roughage he gathered by slitting open a panel of his down jacket, leaving that panel a little leaner than it had been that afternoon.

The tiny owls ate like Roman senators at an orgy. Chaucer seemed to be so amazed that he sailed down again to watch the proceedings from the man's shoulder, and then walked up to the top of the man's head for a better view.

As the man fed the owlets, he clucked to them and talked to them, first apologizing for the lack of mouse meat, and then telling them all sorts of interesting facts about their eyesight and hearing, their population density in the region. He started to go into their mating cycle, but stopped, laughing, and promised them they could hear about that when they were a little older. At long last, they'd had enough—first one, then the other, began nodding sleepily and ignoring the proffered bits of feather-wrapped meat.

The man tucked the tired infant owls back under his pullover and sat down. The tingling of relief to his legs and back reminded him that he'd been on his feet since two o'clock in the afternoon. He said to Chaucer, who'd returned to perch on his shoulder, "Why don't you make me a sandwich, you old feather duster?"

Chaucer walked down his arm, the razor-sharp talons daintily applied, and stepped off to stand on the table, blinking first one intense saucerlike eye, then the other.

The man stretched one graceful, supple-fingered hand and scratched the owl behind the ears, chuckling softly, and then yawned and closed his eyes for a moment . . . man and wild creature in a still tableau. . . .

The silence was broken when he opened his eyes again and looked at his watch, giving a soft curse. He was due soon at work.

The nestlings didn't like much being taken from next to his skin and put back into the box, even though he made them as comfortable as he could. He carried the box up the great staircase to his bedroom and left it there with the door closed. There was no point in testing Chaucer's patience. Then he collected fresh clothes from the drying room near the kitchen, stripping off his hiking clothes and pulled on clean wheat-colored jeans, leather boots, and a V-necked white sweatshirt.

To Chaucer, sitting on the edge of the laundry basket examining a clothespin in one claw, the man remarked, "You probably wonder, don't you, old son, why I never talk about what I do to support us all?" The owl began chewing thoughtfully on the clothespin, giving him a wise look. "The truth is, there's no intelligible way to explain it. Humans have particularly odd forms of entertainment. But it pays what we need to support this rockpile, and now we have two new mouths to feed."

The man pulled on his jacket again and strode out through the new snow to an old station wagon, whistling resignedly.

Jennifer Hamilton, the woman who had faked flu in high school for the entire two weeks her class had studied reproductive biology, the woman who had almost expired with embarrassment in a college art history class when asked to speak on the merits of Michelangelo's David—Jennifer Hamilton, who'd spent a lifetime of twenty-three years misplaced in an era of sexual liberation, was about to attend a club where men took off their clothes to music.

From the outside, the Cougar Club had a deceptive coziness, like a family restaurant that serves fish fries on Friday nights. Inside was another story. Inside it wasn't frying fish that sizzled. It was the stage act.

In fact, Jennifer hadn't realized until she was actually within the friendly white clapboard walls that the place was anything more than the popular nightclub which her four companions, in a spirit of gleeful mischief, had represented it to be. Light had begun to dawn for her when she saw the gift shop just within the front door which merchandised Cougar Club nightshirts and bumper stickers decorated with a provocative male silhouette. There were even more provocative items such as calendars featuring Cougar Club dancers in throat-tightening stages of undress, and a mysterious piece of equipment called a "go-naked pen."

Turning to her companions, trying to look like a woman who thought this was all a good joke instead of one who was likely to require being removed from the place on a stretcher, Jennifer had said, "I can see that I've been grossly misled!"

Her words brought laughter because none of the four women with her had known her long enough to realize that after one glance at the club's logo, an undraped male silhouette, Jennifer's stomach felt as though it had begun to solidify. And because she didn't want to look like a poor sport, it was the last thing she wanted them to discover. She had been in Emerald Lake only two weeks working at her new job as children's librarian at the public library. New job, new town, new people.

She knew it was partly her own fault, but in her home town where she'd lived from birth through college, her acquaintances and neighbors had recognized only her stiff, rather formal exterior. But another wider and more playful soul had grown beneath that exterior . . . and it had such a difficult time showing itself.

Jennifer had come at Annette's invitation tonight. Annette, a tall friendly woman, was adult services librarian. Somehow she accomplished a remarkable amount in spite of the impression she gave of always being on the way to the back room to have a cigarette. Annette's younger sister Diane had come also, and her friend Susan. They were leaning over the merchandise counter, wearing straight-leg jeans, blouson jackets and boots with heels, looking like a page from the Spiegel catalogue. Lydia beside them was the library aide.

She had just picked up a logoed G-string and was giving it the twice over.

Taking it from her with a twinkle in her eyes, Annette said, "What do you think? Should I buy one of these for the hubby?"

Susan laughed. "C'mon. Bill would never put on one of those things."

"Little do you know Bill's private side," Annette said. "He'd have it on in two minutes."

With a grin and a teasing push on the arm, Diane said, "And you'd have it off again in one!"

Annette picked out a calendar and paid a woman who happened to be pregnant and was wearing a Cougar Club T-shirt; as was the girl behind the counter at the coat-check stand; as was the female maître d'. Jennifer found herself wondering in an unnerved way if any of this was in some way connected with the nature of the entertainment provided inside. She was further unnerved by the press of women who were departing, flushed and ecstatic, from the previous show. One clapped her on the back and said,

"Whew! En-*joy!*"

As they walked into the packed cavern of the nightclub, Jennifer looked through the candles flickering on many tables to the ominous, empty stage dominating the room. She turned to Annette.

"I see a free table in the back corner—"

"Oh, no," Annette said with a wolfish smile. "I should think we'd want to sit fairly close."

"*Very* close," put in Diane.

They ended up directly in front of the stage, which was raised just enough to put anyone on it at thigh level with Jennifer's nose. Generously, her friends insisted she take the closest seat. When she protested in a suffocated voice that it might kill her, they thought she was being witty.

Admission was for women only. It was an attractive crowd that ran the gamut of ages, though the concentration seemed to be of women in their twenties and thirties. And not one of them would have looked out of place in a meeting of the local PTA or at church choir practice. They were letting down their hair with the weekend-away-from-home exuberance of farm implement salesmen at a convention. The young male waiters—who seemed to hail from that class of folks know as "hunks" —were receiving some pretty risque answers when they came to the tables collecting orders for drinks, asking, "What would you like?"

The waiters responded to the ribald answers with quick, accustomed smiles, and brought them drinks instead. Their waiter, who introduced himself as Rick, couldn't quite repress a gleam of interest, though, when Diane leaned her elbows on the table. Her long blond hair trailing forward over her red ribbed sweater, she asked, "For the fifteen dollar cover charge, do I get to take you home too?"

Mounting the stage wearing a clinging knit dress, the Mistress of Ceremonies had geranium-red lips and looked like she'd have become someone's mistress without too much ceremony. There was a slight, intriguing hard edge to the lean, beautiful woman. Her hair, long and black, caught the smoky light from the spots like vintage Cher Bono as she welcomed the audience.

"Ladies who come here are usually celebrating something," she observed, and looked around the room, randomly choosing tables, asking for the occasion. There was a doe party for a young girl who was getting married in a week; a group of student nurses who'd gotten their caps; a woman leaving for the Air Force. One divorce. (A burst of sympathetic cheers. The M.C. sent over a certificate for free drinks on the house.) There was also a busload of bank employees from Chicago. They were toasting the night with margaritas, in a way that would probably have started a stampede of investors withdrawing their money if any of them had been there to see it.

"Illinois girls know how to party *hard*!" The M.C. grinned. "And that's good. Let's take a poll, ladies. How many of you have never seen any man besides your husband or your boyfriend in the altogether? Let's see your hands!"

Many hands rose. But not Jennifer's. Jennifer's hands had welded themselves to the sides of her chair.

"Enlightenment awaits!" promised the M.C. in high good humor. "Tonight you're going to see *everything* of three gorgeous guys and find out how the men in your lives"—she winked—"measure up!"

Amid the howling approval around her, Jennifer tried to sink as low as possible in her chair without disappearing under the table; she spared a thought for her poor mother, receiving the news that her only child had suffered a fatal heart attack in a nightclub featuring male strippers.

She made it halfway through the first act. But when the macho hunk onstage five feet from her dropped his hands to the waistband of his skintight glitzy slacks, and made teasing motions that indicated he was going to divest himself of them, she vanished into the restroom.

Feeling like an idiot, and a coward, and a mouse creeping out of a knothole, she emerged when the music and explosion of whistling and foot-stomping applause had faded into the lower roar of excited conversation that signalled the end of the first act.

A waiter taking drink reorders from the table of graduate nurses blocked the narrow path to her table. Standing patiently, listening with a reddening ear to the M.C.'s bawdy routine, she heard a woman seated nearby say, "Deb, look at that—the guy who just came out to change the tape. Is he *cute!*"

As she turned her head to the array of sound equipment edging the stage, Jennifer was wondering mildly how women could bring themselves to go into ecstasies over another of these vacuous, beef-on-the-hoof jocks. Then her gaze lit upon the tall blond man in wheat jeans and a white sweatshirt, who stood by the sound table with a tape in his hand.

Never had she seen a face like this one. Carved in simple planes, it contained a strict beauty that carried no trace of prettiness. His hair had the diffuse brightness of sunlight pouring through spring water. Under sable eyebrows, a dark fringe of straight lashes defined eyes of haunting crystalline blue. Small smile lines framed a wide mouth. The pure facial structure gave the indelible impression of strength, intelligence and a certain refined tenderness—it was a face built for sweetness. But the brooding eyes were a cynic's. He was here, yet remote from all this; detached. That, and the straight classical proportions below made him look like a statue of the young Alexander.

Jennifer heard the woman seated in front of her who'd been addressed as Deb breathe, "What a babe!" While Jennifer disapproved of the extravagant phrasing, she had to admit to some echo of the sentiment inside herself. Here was the expected coronary, but caused by a man who was fully clothed. With a flash of humor, she thumped a fist lightly against her chest and said, "Pump, heart, pump."

Her own record with men was not what anyone would call impressive. In her dreams she was brave, polished, even a little wild. In reality, she was a worrier. No one ever worried the way she could. It was the one thing she did really well. And because one of the things she worried the most about was men, there she had erected her strongest defenses. Not a prickly person, she was prickly with men. She wasn't good with them. She just wasn't. Attractive males, with their lavish egos, ruffled her the most. Perhaps it was because she was such a plain daisy herself. With her brown hair and brown eyes, she was the very fabric of average. She had a face right off a Norman Rockwell *Post* cover, the picture of wide-eyed Americana. It was a sincere face, at times even a merry one, but in a crowd heads had never turned to look at it.

She was threading through the cleared path to her table when one of the nurses interrupted the M.C. by calling out playfully, "Hey! Is the blond guy going to take off his clothes?"

Jennifer watched him pretend to ignore the remark as he wound the tape, his broad mouth stretched in a smile that suggested he might be laughing inside.

Mock-indignant, the M.C. made a "naughty-naughty" sign with her index finger. "Have you no shame? The poor kid is barely seventeen years old—" Laughing protests and a suggestive comment or two around the room greeted the obvious fiction. Jennifer would have put his age at perhaps a year or two older than her own. Grinning, the M.C. continued, "I'm ashamed of you ladies and your carnal intentions. And in front of a minor! Anyway, he's only the sound man, so—behave! Because I've got something here for all of you who luh-hu-uvv"—she gave the word three syllables—"law and order: a tribute to our gentlemen in blue! Here's a man you'd love to go undercover with. For your entertainment pleasure, allow me to present Peter the Policeman!"

Jennifer landed in her seat just as a magnificent body in a motorcycle cop's outfit—with silver helmet, shiny black knee-length leather boots, reflecting aviator sunglasses—landed onstage inside a swell of acclaim. Moving at full throttle and with dynamic professionalism to the theme from *Peter Gunn*, he was a riveting figure. If she hadn't known he was about to take his clothes off, Jennifer almost might have enjoyed it.

The aviator shades came off to reveal lustrous black eyes. Beneath the discarded silver helmet was a shining mass of stunning ebony hair and Jennifer swallowed nervously. He slid out of his black leather jacket and began opening his blue shirt. Beneath was a finely muscled chest and taut stomach—Jennifer's palms started sweating. The half-naked policeman began stroking his palms down his midriff in time to the music, his hips moving. To a riot of encouragement, his deft fingers played with the buckle of his wide black belt. Jennifer had slid so low in her chair that her chin was nearly level with the table. But she was not too low to miss the policeman's gesture toward her when it came. Fingering the buckle, crooking the index finger of his other hand invitingly, and looking right at her with a come-to-me smile, he showed her by look, by gesture that he wanted her to join him onstage and unzip his . . . Jennifer choked. The tables around her exploded with excitement and rippling laughter. Embarrassment hit her, so strong that it nauseated her and burned from the top of her head to her shoulders. Her face buried itself in the shelter of her table napkin.

Nor did she emerge. The banter and cheering around her told her that Susan had taken her place. The music evolved to a slower, more sensual beat. Her head came up in involuntary surprise and alarm when she heard Diane cry out,

"Oh, my God, will you look at that? *It glows in the dark!*"

The policeman's G-string, glowing like a beacon in the blacklight, was moving with the supple rotation of his pelvis. The light changed again and she tore her gaze away and to the side—and discovered that the light-haired man at the sound table was watching her. *Yes, her.* The alluring blue eyes were holding her in a level study. As she sat very still, staring numbly back, she began to read in the perceptive depths of his eyes a heart-catching mixture of amusement, sympathy, and interest. For a suspended moment her heart beat

oddly as their gazes touched, and then she dragged
her eyes away.

Looking everywhere in the room except the stage,
in a harried effort to avoid the trauma of finding
out how Peter the Policeman measured up (which
was very well according to the wild response around
her), she had time to wonder how much of what
she had seen in those blue eyes was a trick of her
imagination, or the stage lights, or even their
breathtaking form. Subliminal chemistry was
doing uncomfortable things to the inside of her,
but she told herself it was probably due more to
the awkwardness of all of this than to a direct
response to a man who'd looked at her once. She
was too self-conscious to risk another glance back
toward him until the policeman had left the stage—
out of uniform.

The blond man at the sound console was making an array of adjustments to the apparatus in
front of him, the austere beauty of his hands
outlined against the stark mechanics. The prac-
ticed movements were done by rote; the far-seeing
gaze was softly unfocused as though his thoughts
had drifted elsewhere. Appearing from a door on
stage right, the M.C. laid her hand on his rear
pocket and squeezed gently as she walked by. A
tingle of laughter swept through the audience from
those who had seen it. The M.C. looked back over
her shoulder at the man and his ironical eyes lit
slightly as he gave her a smile of bewitching reproach before leaving the area by a side door.

"Give us the sound man!" came a shout from
the banking group.

The M.C., who had begun to speak, ignored the
interruption, but the call for the blond man spread

like a chant through the crowded room. Encouraged by a certain gleam in the M.C.'s grin, the clamor grew in momentum. More and more voices joined the swell. Raucous whistles rocketed toward the stage. Rhythmic clapping erupted. Breaking into laughter, motioning the rebels into order, the M.C. had to shout into the microphone to make herself heard.

"All right, all right! Talk about lascivious . . . I can see you've all had the same thought as I did two years ago when I came upon him sitting on the public pier dangling his toes in the lake, his jeans rolled up to his knees. . . ." She chuckled at the thunder of delight before her. "When I look for men to dance in my club, I'm looking for very special ones. They have to have better than good looks. They have to have better than good dancing ability. I go way beyond that. I look for men with that unique charisma that—well, you know what it does to you. As you've guessed, he's not the sound man, he's definitely not a minor and he definitely *is* the showpiece of the Cougar Club! Ladies, the Cougar Club is proud to present the number one male dancer in the Midwest. Here he is, our own native blueblood to make your blood simmer—"

Amid pandemonium, and Jennifer's confusion because she had not really guessed that the blond man with the gentle gaze and face like a vision would strip off his clothes for money, he strolled onstage to the beat of "Stray Cat Strut." It seemed profane. It seemed like Michelangelo's David leaping down from his pedestal and performing a bump and grind on the Accademia Di Belle Arti floor.

And yet bump and grind this was not. He was a

whimsical blue-collar fantasy in a light shiny hardhat. A form-fitting red plaid shirt molded to his upper body, leading the eyes irresistibly downward into the softly faded denim caressing his hips and long thighs. The pounding rhythm loved his hard body. There was a mesmeric quality, an almost playful kinetic energy to his natural grace. Moving to the music with easy sensuality, he pulled off the hardhat in a flow of athletic choreography. The light hair tumbled sensuously, and the blue and hot-silver eyes held a laughter that was at the same time innocent and full of utter deviltry.

"God, he's so . . ." murmured Annette.

The quaking excitement inside Jennifer had nothing to do with embarrassment, though heaven knew she was embarrassed by what she saw, by what she felt. The icy ball that her stomach had become was melting all down the inside of her, through her nerves, into pumping pathways that led downward, inward.

He drew a woman from the eager audience. She came easily to him, and basking her in the flood of his radiant gaze, he lifted her hand gently to the top button of his shirt. Holding her smaller hand cupped inside his against his chest, he guided her hand slowly lower, and the buttons fell open as he moved himself, and her, to the music that had grown softer. Soft too was the brush of a finger under her chin, tipping up her face for a lingering kiss.

He let one arm shrug out of the shirt, then more slowly the other, the liquid sway of his hips still catching the beat. Jennifer could almost feel the softness of his bare flesh, the heat and steel that came beneath. Her throat could almost taste the light tang of sweat the traced the intoxicating hollows stretched along his muscles. His vitality projected like rocket fire through the room, burning the imagination, flaming the watching bodies. At the edge of the stage he held out his hand to a woman seated below. When she stood beside the stage, hungry to touch him, he took her wrists in his hands and stirred her palms slowly over his lean hips and the compact satin flesh of his lower stomach. One of his hands slipped into her short curls, dropping her head lightly back to receive his kiss.

Smoky disco and husky harmonics poured over the stage and into the audience as another woman came forward. He carried her hands to his jeans and through the motions of dragging open the snap, dragging down the dense brass ribbon of the zipper, and peeling the pliant cotton fabric lower as though she were unwrapping hard candy.

Now, except for the slight fabric that left him exposed almost completely in back, he was nude. The purity of clean body lines in the ivory spot carried the wattage of chain lightning. The rim of the low stage filled four deep with women waiting breathlessly to tuck a folded dollar into the tiny garment he wore and to kiss the wide, smiling mouth.

Jennifer felt a twist of longing so strong that it made her stomach hurt as she stared hypnotized at his long hands bringing up a trembling chin on a curved forefinger, capturing a face carefully between his palms, his lips parted, parting further over mouths beneath his. Smooth hands reached up to him during the kisses, caressing his shoulders, holding his waist, running daringly over the solid willowiness of his buttocks.

Over the music and boom of room noise, the comments of women returning from the stage were clear.

"Oh God . . . his lips are so soft. . . ."

"He *kisses*—I mean he *really* kisses."

"I could die for a man like that." A laugh. "I'm going to make my husband do this at home."

Diane flopped back in her seat beside Jennifer, throwing one hand over her heart.

"You've been up there twice," Annette said, her eyes sparkling, mirthful.

"I know! I told him I had to come back."

Lydia leaned toward her. "What'd he say?"

"He just laughed. Jennifer, heavens, don't miss it! How often does anyone get a chance to make magic with a man like that?" Diane gave Jennifer a gay little nudge, and Susan, coming back with flushed cheeks and overbright eyes from the stage, tried laughingly to haul Jennifer to her feet. Sticking like a burr to her small wooden chair, thrown further into unfamiliar mental disarray, Jennifer tried feebly, "I'd better not. I . . . think I have a cold coming on and I wouldn't want to—"

The end of her sentence was swallowed up by the laughter of her companions. Lydia was saying, "Fie on you, woman! You haven't either!" when Jennifer, whose eyes had been straying helplessly to the stage for no very good reason, saw that for the second time that evening, the blond man was looking right at her. He must have seen the attempt of her friends to pull her from the chair, and her strong negative reaction, because he released the beautiful young woman he was holding. His head tilted in a pantomime of tenderness and curiosity. And then he beckoned to her, his smile roguish, sensual.

Jennifer's fingers clutched the sides of her chair in a death grip. One corner of his beautiful mouth quirked upward as he gave her a look of humorous reproach. Trying desperately to maintain the little that was left of her dignity, her accustomed air of self-command, she didn't resort to such drastic measures as putting her head back into her palms until she saw, disbelievingly, that if she wouldn't come to him, he was going to come to her. She was beyond being about to control the small moan of distress that rose to her lips, or the fluid rise of heat to her cheeks as she covered them with her hands.

The women around her greeted his action with ecstatic relish, yet his seductive murmur touched her ear with the morning-soft mist of his respiration.

"Hello, lady," he whispered. "Open your eyes." When she would not, he murmured, "I only want to kiss you." She felt the shock of his warm hands gently pulling at her wrists and urging her chin up. Then, not persisting in the face of her frozen resistance, he stroked the outer curve of her hot cheek with a soothing finger, "You know what, lady? I think you're sweet."

She was not able to watch the rest of his act as he abandoned his final cover to Dylan's melodic rasp. The unfeigned lyrics of "Lay, Lady, Lay" seeped through the loudspeakers. But she knew that it was another voice and the light experienced touch of one man that would stay with her through the night.

He came out of the shower into the small room that was supposed to be his private dress-ing room, and found Darrell, in his own clothes now but, in spite of it being three o'clock in the morning, still wearing the aviator shades that had become his trademark as Peter the Policeman. Darrell had arranged himself comfortably on one of the two chairs with his boot up on the other. He moved quickly through to protect his suede jacket from errant water drips as Philip passed him.

"I swear, Philip, you're as bad as a bird dog the way you shake off your hair after a shower," Dar-rell objected. "Listen, I'm going over to Julie's house tonight and—"

"Which Julie?"

"Julie with the Porsche. And I think you ought to come along. Her sister's going to be there; you remember April—"

"Yes. Thanks. But not tonight."

Darrell frowned. "It would do you good to get laid."

The mildly scolding tone amused Philip. Moms and chicken soup. Darrell and sex. "Why?" he asked, though the question was moot, an affec-tionate tease.

Darrell hated to think about the "whys" of anything. He was still looking disgruntled and muttering "What do you mean, *why*?" to no one in particular when Michele poked her head in the door.

"Are you decent?" she asked. She glanced at

Philip standing nude in the middle of the floor toweling his hair, and walked in anyway. It would have been useless to try to evict her, but he knew she would be disappointed if he didn't make the effort so he said, "Is this a private showing or what?"

Michele grinned. "I've already seen you plenty." Kicking Darrell's booted foot off the extra chair, she collapsed in it, lifting the heavy coil of thick black hair tiredly off her neck. Her eyes were awake and genial as she ran them suggestively over his hips and said wickedly, "After all this time it's no big thing to me." After his laughter, "You were good tonight."

He began to pull on his jeans. "You say that every night."

"You're good every night." She withdrew a somewhat crushed menthol cigarette from her cleavage and stuck it between her lips. "I don't get it. Here you get a visit from this talent guy from Hollywood" —she paused, inhaling as Darrell applied his lighter, "and you tell him no."

It was difficult to make them understand and to avoid a familiar argument, he said, "I can't leave. Darrell would get too lonely."

Darrell gave him a disapproving stare over the top of the aviator shades and glanced back at Michele. "I think he's getting weird living alone in that crazy old place. I swear, it looks like the door ought to be opened by some guy with a bump on his back and one eye higher than the other named Igor."

Michele spit a rush of smoke and laughter. When she was able to choke out an answer to Darrell's demand to know what was so funny, she gasped, "What was the name of the other one?"

"Huh?"

"If Igor was the name of"—laughing pause—"of one eye, then what's the n-name of the other eye?" One look at Darrell's face brought on a fresh burst that ended with a coughing fit. She waved her hand and said placatingly, "I'm sorry. Never mind. I'm getting punchy. Anyway, it wasn't all you. I was just remembering that little chick in the first row—the one with the Dorothy Hamill hair who kept trying to disappear into her napkin. When Philip's pants came off I thought we might have to administer oxygen to the chick."

Darrell pocketed his lighter. "Chick's probably never been with a man in her life."

Amused by the censure in Darrell's tone that implied the lady was being strongly negligent in her responsibility toward the male sex, Philip's thoughts wandered back to her . . . the gleaming brown hair, the bashful eyes, the dusty-rose lips which had fallen slightly open over straight white teeth, the front one slightly chipped. He recalled having the vague urge to stroke the uneven outline there with his tongue, and for the first time that night he felt a rush of desire. Strange, because he rarely paid attention to individuals in the sea of faces and this one hadn't been particularly striking except perhaps for the brown eyes that had been so filled with personality. He had a sudden memory of her soft flesh under his searching fingers, the firm cheek round and blush-heated.

"Philip? Something wrong?" Michele was staring at him, her narrow face set in the tense way it did when she found him unusually cryptic.

"No." He smiled at her and bent to kiss her goodnight as he buttoned his shirt. "Thanks again, Darrell. Tell April and Julie—"

"I know." Darrell gave him a long-suffering look. "Another night."

The air outside was crystalline, carrying the tranquil scent of the fresh snowfall that glazed the birch branches near the club's back door and spread like a skirt of moonlight over fields and rooftops. It was icy cold. Clean. And he breathed it deeply. Things were not as bad for him as they had been at first. The feeling of being vaguely revolted with himself had passed as Michele had predicted it would. He had come to accept it, and that was neither bad nor good. It was necessary.

Chaucer met him at the mansion door. He climbed the wide staircase in the darkness with the owl on his shoulder, pausing for a moment on the first landing. Gazing out the huge windows at the black, star-sprinkled sky and the pristine expanse of the lake, he thought of the girl who had refused his kiss and said softly, "I want you in my bed, brown eyes."

The owl stirred and when he glanced at its starlit face, it gave him a slow wink.

The baby owls were ready to be fed again and by now he was weary. But he was also disciplined, and so he fed the orphans, and when they were full, put them back into the shoebox and set that into an armchair wedged against his bed. If they woke up and managed to clamber out of the box, he didn't want them tumbling to the floor.

Tired as he was, he read *Nicholas Nickleby* for

half an hour to wind down. Reaching over to turn out the light, he found himself face to beak with the owlets who had scrambled up on his pillow. They were staring intently at him, side by side, twin puffballs with eyes the color of spring dandelions.

"Doubles, anyone?" he said, and reached up to tickle the breast feathers of one, then the other. "You're cold, I suppose?" He raised himself on his elbow. "I'm going to lay the cards on the table with you two. I'm a human who studies raptors. You, by the way, are raptors, which is why I happen to know how to take care of you. I'm very sorry to have to tell you this, but I'm not your mother. There are limits to what you should expect." They toddled closer to his warmth. "This is really beneath my dignity. I have an advanced degree, you know." The yellow eyes, shining at him like four tiny moons, held no more awe of him than Chaucer's ever had. With a sigh, he lifted an edge of the cover. "All right, come on. Just this once."

The babies scurried down into the warm hollow beside his body and he carefully dropped the cover again.

"Don't get used to this. When you're old enough I'm going to rehabilitate you to the wild."

They were cuddled up with their heads on his arm as he drifted to sleep.

Two

Dear Mom,

Things are going so well at the library that it's hard to keep that "new job" caution. Mrs. Paynter the library director is quite charming. She collects fossils, paints in a lively primitive style that reminds me of Grandma Moses and, at least once a day, the library and staff are thrown into chaos hunting for her lost glasses. While she doesn't like to initiate new ideas herself, she doesn't seem to mind if the rest of us do. I've already added gerbils to the children's section, and I'm meditating upon a good place to set up an aquarium.

Annette, the adult librarian, has been a tremendous help. I can't wait until you meet her. What a ball of fire! Very foxy for a librarian too. She has a younger sister—Diane Dorst—you may have heard of her; she models in New York. Diane flew in last Thursday for a week of vacation and yesterday I spent the day with Annette, Diane, one of Diane's friends from high school, and Lydia, who's one of the library aides (and rather tart of tongue, but good-hearted underneath). In the late afternoon they drove me around Emerald Lake and we looked at the wonderful old mansions built by Chicago millionaires a hundred years ago as summer homes for their families. The names are amazing—they rival Lake Geneva with its Wrigleys, Chalmerses, and Sears. Many were hidden from the road by trees, including Lily Hill, belonging to the Brooks family, which the local history books claim was the showplace of the Midwest in its time. But I saw enough to have visions of ladies with frilly parasols crossing green shaded lawns while little boys in knickers and girls with huge hair ribbons rolled hoops on gravel pathways, their proud papas watching from the verandas. Did I tell you that their mail was, and still is, delivered by a boat? Just like *On Golden Pond*. Some of the mansions have remained in the family, though Annette said even the rich can't live on quite the same scale anymore.

After the lake tour we had quiche at Annette's, of which she said (tartly of course) we didn't have to worry about eating it, not being real men. Which leads neatly into the subject of men.

You'd never guess where they took me afterward. To see male strippers. No kidding. And they take off *everything. Every stitch.* Can you believe this is legal in Wisconsin? Or that you'd find it in a small town like Emerald Lake? Actually most people in town don't frequent the place. The clientele is affluent, mainly youngish, and from Milwaukee and Chicago and the resort areas around Lake Geneva, even though it's quite a drive. Of course you want to know how your only begotten child bore up in the face of naked men. Not well. However, I did see the most handsome man in the world. Yes. It's true—there *is* a most handsome man in the world and he lives in Emerald Lake. Do you remember the bust of Alexander the Great we saw in the Getty Museum last summer? This was him. So now I know what Alexander looked like from the neck down, too. You know how one sometimes reads a description of someone as having an aristocratic appearance, and you think (in a down-to-earth American way) tch-tch, what's aristocratic? This man looked aristocratic, and here he was, taking off his clothes for money. And you just knew he was the kind of man who drives a Corvette, wears aviator shades—and has a huge poorly trained German shepherd who barks at company and tries to poke his nose in your crotch. Dreams die hard. Mind you, I could have kissed this guy but I was too embarrassed. You know me. However, no one thought the worse of me for being timid about it all. They thought I was joking.

> I love you,
> Jennifer

P.S. I've finally had a piña colada. Interesting stuff. I may have more.

Five days after she'd dropped the letter to her mother into a friendly blue box marked U.S. MAIL,

Jennifer stood at the library window, her elbows on the window ledge, her chin in her hands, her legs against the radiator's warm teeth. The Wisconsin outside was a Christmas card. She could see Emerald Lake stretching flat and frozen to the stark trees on the distant white shore. Iceboats skimmed far out on the lake under colorful sails, and nearby, teenagers walked mitten in mitten along the lakepath, past young mothers pulling sledloads of small children bundled into shapes like teddy bears under their layers of winter clothing. The clear, crystal-free black ice of the nearby cove was beginning to fill with ice-skaters let out of school at three-thirty. Red and yellow pompoms shone bright on skate laces, polished blades swept in swirls and figure eights, shaving foamy ice-dust from a scarring surface. Her imagination could hear the laughter and shouts that the window glass silenced.

This was life, a thing she watched happening from the other side of a clear pane while she hung back and hung back, guarding the brave dreamer inside. She took no risks, and that gave her quiet, safety . . . and restlessness.

The sun was low above the hills behind the lake, a swollen wreath of fiery white, the emblem of one more fading day. The afternoon had been still and to her right an elderly gentleman had nodded asleep behind a newspaper. The long rectangles of sunlight from the back windows crept imperceptibly across the brown carpet between the stacks.

Soon the after-school crowd would fill the round pine tables around her with their landslide of homework questions, and she would be too busy to stand by the window thinking of laughing blue eyes and a beckoning hand that each time brought a hard lifting sensation inside her stomach.

She looked back over her shoulder as Mrs. Paynter sailed around the corner, her black silver-stranded hair straggling, her sensible shoes library-soft on the floor, her arms filled with clipboards and rolled posterboard. Spying Jennifer, she said, "Ah, here you are! I knew you were going to take your break but I assumed you take it in the back room. . . . Have you seen what Annette's done back there now? I walked in to have my lunch, sat down on the desk, and found myself practically cheek to cheek with an unclothed man. The cheek I contributed was on my face. His was not!"

Divining that Mrs. Paynter was referring to the Cougar Club calendar, Jennifer diplomatically suggested, "Maybe it's art."

"Art! If that young man had been a woman, he would have been a hussy. Naked is naked, even if they have him posed so you can't see his ding-dong."

Jennifer's eyes flew wide and she tried to disguise her eruption of laughter as a rather unsavory episode of choking.

Mrs. Paynter was not deceived. "I'd like to know what you call it then."

Hastily, with a spreading grin, Jennifer said, "Oh, nothing at all. I do everything I can to avoid the subject entirely. I'm not much of a . . ." She found it necessary to clear her throat, and the grin died. *Well, come on, Jennifer, what is it that you're not much of? A woman, perhaps?* An odd bitter thought. Was that what watching life through a window did to you? Did it make you increasingly odd, more bitter? Either she must learn to accept herself as she was or she must learn to be more open to life. More open—wasn't that what she was doing by moving to Emerald Lake, living in a new community, nourishing new friendships? *Yes. I'm starting. So don't panic.* Impatient that she had caught herself worrying again, she dropped the unfinished sentence and gave the raft of posters in Mrs. Paynter's arms an interested look.

"What have you got there?"

"Publicity for the fund drive!" Rearranging the motley collection of paper, Mrs. Paynter unearthed a poster, rolled off a thick red rubber band and opened the poster with a flourish. "Every year we try to work around some inspirational little phrase. This year we've chosen TAKE THE DUMB OUT OF FREEDOM, and as you can see, we've used an Abe Lincoln motif."

Jennifer studied the Lincoln motif, trying to look inspired. On the poster, Lincoln stood beside a log cabin, his head a copy of the penny profile. Gear-shaped snowflakes flew around his hapless figure. Under his arm he was holding a book labeled "Shakespeare" that looked as big as a suitcase, and big bare toes like Snuffy Smith's adorned feet blue with cold.

"It's very . . ." Corny. Jennifer dragged out the hesitation, nodding thoughtfully, but she wasn't proof against the latent anxiety in Mrs. Paynter's earnest face. "Very nice. I take it you've sort of based things on the story about Lincoln walking barefoot through a blizzard for miles to return a book he'd borrowed. Since this month is his birthday?" More nodding. "Ah-*huh.* Very clever."

"I'm so glad you think so!" Mrs. Paynter said, beaming. "Annette and Lydia didn't seem to care for it at all."

Unhappily, Jennifer found herself in the position of having to spend the next few minutes hypocritically pshawing Annette's very astute criticisms. Hasty to abandon that unprincipled role, she said, "I'd be more than pleased to help out, if you need any extra bodies."

"Why, isn't that kind. We rely for most of our support on our Friends of the Library group—saints, all of them—but I've got a two-hour slot on Saturday that—let me see . . ." The stack clutched in her arms teetered, threatening an avalanche as she excavated her clipboard and gazed myopically at the top page and then said, "My glasses! Don't tell me I've mislaid—"

"They're on the top of your head, Eleanor."

"Oh yes"—retrieving them—"thank you. Are you busy on Saturday afternoon from one to three?"

"No. That'll be great," Jennifer agreed, imagining a few pleasant hours spent painting posters or making telephone calls. She was more than a little unsettled ten minutes later when Annette stopped by her desk to hand her the latest *Publisher's Weekly*, and said, "Be busy Saturday afternoon. Eleanor may try to con you into donating an hour toward the fund drive."

"I've already signed up for two hours. Why not?"

"Oh, how they prey on the young and innocent," Annette said dryly, gazing skyward. "Kid, make it a resolution never to volunteer for anything again until you've found out what it is."

•   •   •

Saturday afternoon at two o'clock Jennifer stood, an icicle, in front of a small boutique on the corner of Emerald Lake's busy shopping thoroughfare.

A top hat teetered on her head, threatening to envelop her eyebrows, and over two layers of thermal underclothes, she wore a sober-hued frock coat, a high collar and starched cravat, a long waistcoat, and woolen trousers that were rolled up at the cuff to keep them from dragging on the icy street. The Lincoln motif.

On one side of her was a rather optimistically large papier-mâché log cabin with a slot in the roof for contributions. When someone tossed in a donation, she was supposed to pull a string that was rigged to release a puff of dry ice smoke from the tin chimney. On her other side, on a stand, was an old schoolbell that Eleanor had painted with a crack and the words "Let Freedom Ring." She was supposed to ring the bell to attract attention, which was not something she had any great desire to do despite her determination to be a good sport. The bell's toll in the frigid sunlit air was sharp and loud and she hardly would have been surprised if they could hear it all the way to Philadelphia.

She was squinting up into a cold bright sun when a snowball came spinning past her head and disintegrated against the brick wall behind her. She ducked, but a second missile carried off her top hat. Her short hair swirled in an icy gust of wind as she swung around looking for her attacker. A little crew of children peeked, giggling, around the corner of the bank three doors down, their eyes glowing above scarves, below stocking caps.

"Darn it all!" Irritation warred with a strong desire to laugh. "So. Munchkins." She bent to pick up her hat, dusting off the snow, and the small faces disappeared, probably manufacturing more ammo. A smile blossomed as she swept up a handful of snow and packed it good. She tossed it discreetly up and down behind her back until she saw the line-up of small faces peer cautiously out. She took three running steps toward them. The children scattered, shrieking excitedly as she let fly with her snowball.

It never came within ten feet of them. Instead it whacked full force into the sleeve of an expensive suede jacket on one of two men who had chosen this particularly bad moment to emerge from the bank. Dismayed, she began to call out, "I beg your pardon!"

The words perished in her throat. Beneath the suede jacket were the magnificent shoulders and narrow waist that she had last seen as Peter the Policeman. Dark snapping eyes behind leather-trimmed aviator glasses were glaring at her. At his side, not quite as tall, but infinitely more graceful in a light cream-colored cotton parka and heather gray wool pants that were cut more for comfort than to show off the exquisite contours underneath, was the man whose image could control the rhythm of her heart.

He had seen her too. The sweet-cruel eyes had begun to fill with interest, amusement, and to her horror what appeared to be a dawning recognition. It was impossible surely that in so many people, over so many nights, he would have retained her image—but he was coming toward her. With her pulse thumping, she backed up quickly until the brick wall at her back slammed her to a stop. The stovepipe hat fell forward onto the bridge of her nose.

Strong hands in cashmere gloves pulled her out from the wall and, with a slow, careful movement, resettled her hat. Sky-blue eyes smiled into hers. The warm mist of his breath caressed her lips. Natural light made him more real, much more man than ornament. No dream held her, but a forceful human being. Smothering in his nearness, she missed the approach of the other man until he spoke.

"Friend of yours, Philip?" The tone was filled with disdain, and, twisting to look at the handsome face above the suede jacket she encountered the look she was most accustomed to receiving from very good-looking men: dismissal. But instead of dwelling on that discovery, she thought disjointedly that she knew the blond man's name. *Philip.* It was one of those names she could never say without imagining it written in longhand in Spencerian script as though it belonged to some Elizabethan scholar-playwright.

"I'd know this worried brow anywhere." Philip drew off his own light wool muffler and teasingly covered the part of her face that her own hands had hidden recently at the Cougar Club. "No doubt about it. Same lady."

She recognized his accent. The diction was upper-class, but softened by a lack of either emphasis or affectation. It was the type of voice her mother called Midwest Patrician, and it clearly didn't match his profession. That profession and all the circumstances of their previous meeting were strong in her mind as she tried to assert herself in a situation that was inherently flattening. His light touch felt like a capture.

"Look," she said to the open space between the two men, "I'm sorry about the snowball,"—especially if you think I threw it at you to attract your attention, she added mentally—"but you see, there were four children . . ." who naturally by now had vanished. Her eyes were drawn irresistibly back to Philip, whose face carried nothing to indicate whether he thought the children were fictitious, or even that it mattered. He was smiling at her in a way she couldn't fathom, a way she found immensely threatening.

She had no idea what to expect next, so she was startled when he took the muffler and began to arrange it with care around her neck. The fleecy fiber held his body's warmth, and the soft cashmere of his gloves brushed underneath her chin on skin made hypersensitive by the cold. Bittersweet shocks of reaction wavered through her upper body and compressed her chest, and she inhaled a stinging lungful of chilled air as his hands lightly covered her cheeks, gently massaging them. Filled with strangled pleasure, she was so taken aback that she couldn't immediately frame the words to make this bewildering attention stop.

Rubbing the back of his forefinger gently up and down the wind-pinked length of her nose, he asked, "Have you recovered from your exposure to the show the other night? Maybe I should say, from my exposure to you."

She choked.

"It didn't appear to be exactly your cup of tea," he said. "What's your name?"

"Jennifer Hamilton." The sound of her own name

brought her abruptly to her senses, or at least what she hoped were her senses. The wall behind her hampered a dignified retreat, so she jerked herself sideways to escape his hands and almost collapsed backward over the log cabin. His firm grip cradled her waist, steadied her, then released her, and he took one step backward, too.

His expressive gaze lit briefly on the Lincoln fund drive poster. "Are you a librarian?"

"Yes," she said tersely, her confusion narrowing into a harried wariness.

"I have such fantasies about librarians. If I'd known that last week at the show . . ." His voice was soft, his half-smile slow, direct. "Why wouldn't you let me kiss you?"

Draped against the bricks, waiting impatiently, the man in the suede coat had begun to develop a smirk. Pitiless. They were both pitiless, spoiled, much-sought-after macho hunks who were finding some sadistic entertainment in tormenting an awkward, bashful girl. But this shaken victim was not as defenseless as she seemed. Why wouldn't she let him kiss her? he had asked.

"I thought it might not be a good idea," she snapped. "I'm allergic to penicillin."

The words were not meant to be friendly, but as these things always happened, they sounded considerably worse aloud. His bright gaze held hers, never wavering. He even smiled. And when the man in the suede coat said, "Does she mean? . . ." he answered in an even tone, "She's afraid I might give her a social disease."

The words were light, ironic rather than bitter, betraying none of the private sentiments beneath. The smile had grown wider, infinitely more dan-

gerous, when he said, "Don't worry, Jennifer
Hamilton. They give me a patch test once a week.
So this is going to be perfectly safe." A dollar
came out of his jacket pocket, and before she had
guessed what he was going to do, he had tucked
it into her waistband.

"A donation," he said. "I give kisses for them—do
you?"

Instinct warned her before he moved to take
her, and she was stumbling backward when his
hands closed on her shoulders and drew her close.
She could feel the hard lineup of their thighs, the
crush of her belly and breasts against his yielding
jacket that tightened to their shape. Her gaze was
caught helplessly in his, lotus petals swirling in a
blue floodwater, and she was paralyzed everywhere.
Her respiration grew shallow, a faint warm pressure against lips parting slowly in wonder at the
caressing expectation flowering within her. And
she knew that in spite of everything she wanted
him, wanted this kiss. His hand was moving gently
around her neck, moving upward, cupping and
tilting the back of her head, his fingers spreading
deliciously through her hair. Ermine-soft in cashmere, his little finger stroked dainty tremors into
her spine.

His mouth descended to hers with throat-stop-
ping languor, his eyes holding her entranced until his dark-tipped lashes drifted closed, veiling
the brightness. And her eyes closed too, and as
his breath swirled lightly with hers, she took a
quick, fearful inbreath, and then in the darkness
felt his lips come against hers, hardly touching.
Her heartbeat hammered in her throat, in her
head, and she let his tightening grip press her

hips into his thighs and she burned there, and on her mouth where he was pressing the cool satin of his lips. His breath warmed her cheeks and chin as his tongue followed the modeling of her lips before touching into her mouth with gentle force. And through her body she could feel the scoring heat of it as his hand pushed up on her lower back and bottom, making her slide against him.

When at last he pulled back from her, her numbed gaze wandered over his face, the vivid eyes, the mouth, deliciously damp from her. His hand, which had been cupping the back of her hair, slipped underneath her jaw, cradling her chin.

"Jennifer Hamilton," he said softly, framing both words as though he were committing them to memory. "You're not going to make this easy, are you?"

Then she was released. As the trance began to shatter around her, she saw in a bewildered way that a straggling crowd had gathered. Next to the hunk in suede stood a third man with dark curling hair and gray eyes. His hands were thrust into his ribbed leather jacket.

"The things I miss by being last to cash my check," the stranger said, directing a droll smile at Philip. "I don't know what in the name of heaven that was about, but it looked damned unpatriotic." He scooped up the stovepipe hat that Jennifer hadn't even realized had fallen from her head, and after subjecting it to a dubious examination, set it gently back on her hair. "When she's not head of state, is she someone?"

"She's someone. Her name is Jennifer Hamilton,"

Philip said, smiling at the gray-eyed man, beginning to walk beside him toward the street. "And I'm going to make her a happy woman."

The gray-eyed stranger turned instantly and gave her a look full of humor and delight, and began to laugh. The man she knew only as Peter the Policeman fell in beside them, and she emerged from the final abrupt stage into reality, into a hurricane of fury.

"Not going to make what easy?" she said, the words passing quietly through kiss-numbed lips. She continued to stare idiotically after his retreating figure. Then she repeated, quite loudly, "Make *what* easy?"

He turned halfway across the street and said, "Us." And she watched him walking backward, gazing at her, until "Peter" took hold of his arm and said plaintively, "For God's sake, Philip, will you be done with that weird chick? What's gotten into you? It's damned embarrassing."

It might have been the audacity of a man who made his living taking off his clothes describing an encounter with her as embarrassing. It might have been the emotional aftershock of the kiss. Or it might have been the certainty that again the blond stripper had made a spectacle out of her. But Jennifer Hamilton, coming to the end of her rope, dashed her hat on the ground and thought, Damn you! You're never going to make me a happy woman! Do you understand? Never!

He had vanished into the crowd.

Long habits of dignity caused her to bend slowly and retrieve her hat, looking neither to the left nor right. Shaken, yet steeled, trying her best to pretend that nothing had just happened and that no one around her had noticed a thing, she turned back to her equipment to make the unsettling discovery that she must have dislodged the smoke mechanism on the log cabin when she had tripped against it. It had been puffing vigorously through-out their embrace. Pride made her remain at her post with a frozen countenance.

It may have been her imagination—but had the contributions picked up a little?

Three

Walking through her front door later, stripping off the frock coat, Jennifer realized that his muffler was still curled around her neck.

It wasn't until noon the next day that the conviction she was a wronged woman began to waver.

By that evening she was facing the unsettling truth. She had overreacted to mild teasing from an extremely attractive man who probably spent the better part of his days in enthusiastically requited flirtations.

Midnight found her watching M*A*S*H reruns and feeling wistful.

The mood persisted throughout the next day, and while she fought against the lowness, it seemed to be growing up and around her. Apprehension tore at her, and that was foolish because nothing was going to happen to her. A chance meeting, a few challenging words thrown out by a man in a temper, a kiss. It had happened, but now it was over. Let the regrets and the sting of it go.

But the internal disquiet became strain. She was nervous as she locked up the library Monday night. There was no reason to be nervous, of course, even though she was alone, because Eleanor Paynter was outside, warming up her Gremlin for their shared ride home. But the building seemed desolate in the dim glare of the security lights. Somewhere in the back reaches of the stacks a display book collapsed with a sharp crash and Jennifer jumped. Half smiling at her private display of nerves, she moved more quickly than usual through the litany of tasks. Turn the "Open" sign to "Closed." Make sure the cash drawer was locked. Unplug the coffee pot. Turn down the heat. Double check to be sure the front door was locked. Unlock the overnight book drop—discovering an accidentally locked book drop seemed to bring out the ferocious in people. She'd seen them leave books on the library's front steps in a rainstorm.

She hurried to the back hallway, dragged her camel stadium coat from the hook and zipped it on quickly, fumbling for the brown tweed mittens from the pocket and pulling the matching cuff hat down over her hair and ears.

The bitter cold outside made her clench her muscles and stamp her feet as she engineered the heavy locks on the service door. Somewhere behind her an engine ran reassuringly. She turned, expecting to race toward the Gremlin. But the Gremlin was gone.

Spent light drifted over the library walls from a distant streetlamp and the reflected gleam of the three-quarter moon on the frozen lake beyond carved out an area from the darkness, like a barely lit stage. And within that stage she saw that the only car in the desolate lot was an aging station wagon. And leaning on the front of it, one leather boot up on the bumper, was the man in the cream-colored parka whom she had seen wearing so much less. She turned to ice in her tracks. Seeing her, he shoved off the bumper and walked toward her.

Unsteady pulses thumped in strange places inside her body but she'd made a resolution the night before while she was brushing her teeth that never again would she let any man back her against a wall. Looking frantically around for Eleanor, she heard herself utter, "Mrs. Paynter . . ."

"Eleanor left when I told her I was here to pick you up. She wasn't averse since she was rushing home to catch 'The Maltese Falcon' on cable."

The attractive voice was matter-of-fact, the stance relaxed. His moonlit features revealed no nuances. Trying to cope with the reality of his sudden appearance, she took one hard sustaining breath, feeding oxygen to her poor besieged brain. Okay, brain, what's going on here? His casual use of the head librarian's first name and his just-as-casual reference to Eleanor's plans for the evening were such a severe check that she could only falter, "Eleanor left? Just like that?"

The sensual features seemed to soften as he studied her. "You've been abandoned to the wolves, darling. She didn't so much as hesitate. It helps, of course, that she's known me since the days my eyebrows didn't reach the top of the checkout counter and I was signing out picture books in crayon."

The inside of her mouth and her throat were

bone dry and stinging in the cold air. She tried to swallow and couldn't. "You just . . . lied to her?"

"No." His smile entered her senses like wine. He moved closer. "I do want to pick you up. You might as well resign yourself and come along passively."

His strong fingers took hold of her upper arm, propelling her toward the car, and she yelped, "Now see here. . . ."

"I intend to. But not until you're sitting in the car." Amusement edged the easy voice. "I don't want you to freeze the end of your stuck-up little nose."

Though she didn't quite struggle, alarm made her stiffen as he bundled her into the passenger seat of the station wagon, and she was breathing in jerky little gasps as he climbed into the front seat beside her.

"You can't push me around," she said, somewhat inaccurately.

"Oh yes I can. As a matter of fact, I'm probably only one of a long line of people who can push you around."

She made a noble attempt to pull herself back together. "I have my moments. Of courage, that is."

"Yes indeed." He shoved the key into the ignition and turned to face her, one long shapely denim-clad leg resting on the driveshaft hump. "If you recall I was treated to one of them on Saturday. It was very impressive."

Her gaze had wandered somehow to his mouth, and a strange feeling began to float inside her. She looked straight at him. "Is that why you're here? Do you plan on doing something horrible to me for revenge?"

A touch of his hand turned on the overhead light, shutting the world outside to a distant blackness, shutting her in a flare of glossy yellow light with this utterly beguiling stranger. His face was tilted slightly as he studied her, a slow smile teasing at the corners of his blue eyes. One of his hands rested on the steering wheel, the gloved fingers strong and classical in their grace as they curved along the line of the black plastic. He stretched out his hand to rub his index finger once gently under her chin.

"If that's the best fight you can put up when you think something horrible is about to happen to you, I'm going to enroll you in est. Do you know what's in front of us?"

Her heart had given up its weak effort to do anything more than syncopate, and all she knew how to do was handle this strange thing that was happening to her one moment at a time. She pretended to squint out the blank front windshield before she said,

"A dumpster?"

The smile widened briefly. His eyes searched her face. "I scare you, don't I?"

"I can't help it. I wasn't born with much of a backbone. Congenital defect. Go ahead, though —I'm braced. What have we got ahead of us?"

His eyes had become very bright. "A long night."

"And?" she said with acute apprehension.

"I'd like you to spend it with me," he said gently.

With a low moan, she slid downward in her seat, pulling the brown tweed hat down to cover her entire face. She heard his laughter and the changing purr of the engine as the car moved in reverse, dipping into the street. They traveled down Lake Drive. His hand came to her shoulder and rubbed lightly.

"It doesn't matter," he said in a kind tone, "there are other ways to do these things. For example, we could date, if you think that would be reassuring."

Jennifer thought, I'm dreaming all of this. Her voice, muffled by the hat, said, "Date?"

"Date. That phenomenon of human group behavior where you devote a goodly amount of time to wondering what to wear and fixing your hair and I empty the McDonald's cartons out of my car and we both make sure we've had showers and sprayed ourselves with all the appropriate chemicals that the advertising industry assures us we can't do without. We dig up clean sheets and underwear and make sure they don't have any suspicious stains, just in case that's the—I beg your pardon?"

"Nothing." Muffled voice. "I moaned."

"You do that a lot."

"Only around you."

"It's a promising sign," he said. "Where was I?"

"Sheets and underwear."

"Right. Then I pick you up, or we can meet some place if we're trying to be correct and modern, and try to find some way to behave like ourselves and impress each other at the same time. You try not to disagree with my opinions too often so as not to risk bruising the legendary male ego. But you don't want to agree too often either or you might bore me. You know, if you smother under that hat I might find it a little hard to explain."

"Dump my body by the roadside and leave no fingerprints," she advised him, pulling up her hat. The cold air against her hot skin stung. She took a sideways glance at his profile, stark and stunning in the sparse light from the dash. "Go on. While I'm trying to navigate the ticklish straits between being either a threat or a bore . . ."

"You're also thinking, Lord, is this dude going to make a move on me tonight?—which is an important question because you don't want to give in to me too soon because even in this day and age, the double standard is alive and well, though more subtle. On the other hand, if you wait too long, you run the risk that I'll get tired of waiting and move along. In the meantime, I try to figure out when you're ready on the basis of what are probably some very mixed signals." Braking for a stop sign, he turned and gave her a smile that could have baked bread at twenty paces. "So, do you wanna date?"

Dangerous. Oh, this man was dangerous. He was smart as well as beautiful. What a combination. Someday they were probably going to make him president of something. Of all the men she could have so carelessly thrown down the gauntlet toward, she couldn't have chosen worse. Rubbing the slow, erratic pulse in her throat, she tore her gaze from his and stared out the window at a landscape of dark trees, cold sidewalks, and shadowy snow-covered lawns lit in patches by lattice patterns from the television screens that flickered behind drawn curtains.

"You are aware," she said shakily, "that there are a couple of people left who still consider dating a romantic institution?"

"Yes. That's why I'm willing, if it would make you feel more secure."

There was no way on God's green earth that she would ever feel secure within ten miles of this man. She tried to inject some of the frost that twinkled on the side windows into her voice. "Just what do *you* believe in, Mr.—"

"Brooks. Philip. I believe in a lot of things. Do you mean concerning you?"

I can't take it. I can't take it. "Yes."

"I believe in your ruffled hair on my pillow. I believe in your breath on my skin, and in holding your flushed body—"

"Uncle!" she gasped. "Uncle, uncle! *Please.*" She propped her elbow against the car door and dropped her reeling brow into her mittened palm, but her head came up sharply as she realized that the houses had been replaced by a deep silhouette of wind-gnawed trees and dark blue open fields. She turned toward him in alarm. "Where are you taking me?"

"I'm just driving. You haven't told me where you live."

"Oh." She was beginning to feel like a total idiot. "The Victorian Cottage apartments."

"Okay. We can turn ahead."

For an uncertain moment, she studied the smooth flowing hair, the chaste purity of the bone structure, the brilliant eyes. The quivery feelings in her chest persisted. Then she turned forward, watching the road, haloed in the apricot headlight reflection.

"You know," she said, "you could have found much better prey than me."

"I seriously doubt it. You cringe. That's rare."

"I don't cringe!" She felt a sudden, incredulous fury.

"I'm sorry, but you do."

"Damn it, you're sadistic!"

That made him smile. "No. Actually, I'd like to find a way to make you stop cringing."

In an absent gesture, the hand he had loosely draped over the seat back dipped enough to touch her. His thumb slid to the side of her neck, brushing tinglingly into the lowest hairs. The tip of his middle finger discovered the hollow at the back of her neck and lightly stroked. Sparklike prickles raised all over her body and her movement away from his fingers was almost violent.

"I don't want you to touch me. If you think one unfortunate remark of mine justifies your repeated assaults—"

Inspiration failed her as the wagon twisted sharply to the right, slicing through the open gateposts in a barbed-wire fence onto a field access road. The headlights picked out the dapple of withered corn shocks half-buried in drifted snow. Gears scraped, and the wagon rocked to a halt. He faced her, a hand on the seat back, the other on the steering wheel.

"I think it would be much healthier if we didn't have to operate on this level of illusion." Lazy passion glowed in his eyes. "Let's straighten things out. Come here. And in a minute, we'll decide together if it's an assault."

Anger flared inside her, then died into blankness like the sinking glitter of a drained firework. It would be much healthier . . . men had promised her a thing or two in her life. Philip Brooks was the first who had ever promised to make her healthy.

Most puzzling to her, as she found herself drowning in the shadowed glimmer of his eyes, was how close she was to giving him that chance. Somewhere inside her, the mindless struggle grew still. Why, why, why?

In one short sweep of words he had laid bare her lame rebuffs, with their curious residual touches of adolescent hysteria. And it brought her an unlooked for, painful relief, like sharp fresh air washed into a stale passage. And now, making no move to touch her, he watched her face in perfect silence with a patience that seemed as limitless as it was without effort.

The hot-cold pump of embarrassment beat through her. Tears formed, and yet a feathery peace had settled within. When the indelicate tears had been subdued and she was sure that her voice was going to do what she wanted, she said, "I panic around men."

"Tell me." The voice, the patience were a soft invitation.

"I . . . I have to know. Did you come for me tonight for revenge?"

"For telling me you were allergic to penicillin? Not at all. I don't have that kind of energy. Why do you panic around men?"

"I don't know. I'm just not . . ." She grappled briefly for a word, "debonair."

His smile, a startled slash of delight, consumed the word before he began to laugh, an alluring sound, winsome and melodic, kindling to her senses. "I'll admit debonair isn't the adjective that comes most readily to mind. But thank God. Being that well-protected is like living on the cutting edge of a scythe. You can never let anyone too close. I've been like that too much of my life. Tell me, why isn't Jennifer debonair?"

Purling breezes stirred the corn stalks. Crisp blackness held up the stars in broken chains. The night gave the quiet between them the intimacy of a confessional and she folded her hands on the dash and dunked her chin on them, gazing at the bright moon. Tell me, the voice had softly beckoned.

"It's a little hard to say. I didn't grow up with a father and my mother blames that for everything. But I'm not sure. . . . It might be because I never wanted to grow up, you know? When my friends started getting interested in makeup and clothes and . . . and other things, I just kept thinking: It's happening too fast! It's happening too fast! And puberty—" she gave a low disdainful whistle— "puberty was disgusting. I thought it was going to kill me. These crazy things happening to your body and who asked for any of it?" Dear God, I can't believe I just said that. Am I drunk? Falling apart? In suspended animation? Is he a hypnotist?

"I understand that," he said. "A happy childhood, the warm cocoon that splits open slowly and there you are in a world you never expected. Famine. Aging. Competition. Sex. And you think, what am I doing here? I thought this place was going to be safe. You go to sleep in Kansas and wake up in Oz. I don't know if it's any consolation, but as puberties go, yours looks like it was a smashing success."

"Thank you." She blushed slightly. "No one's ever admired my puberty before."

"They have. Trust me." A pause. Then, gently, "Jennifer? Why don't you like to be touched?"

She felt an echo of buried pain and the sudden stomach-tightening awareness of him as a man. He was sweetly, tinglingly close, a motion away, and she squeezed her eyelids tightly shut, feeling the heavy pinprick sensations that anticipated his touch. She lied. "There isn't a reason. It just makes me uncomfortable."

Through the back of her thighs, she felt his shifting weight on the car seat and then the light presence of his arm, slowly stroking on her back.

"Does this make you uncomfortable?" he asked, a soft inflection in his voice.

"Yes." The word barely escaped her dry mouth. She felt the warm sliding pressure of his flesh as his hand followed the outline of her chin and then raised it gently.

"And this?" he whispered against her mouth as his lips found hers with the lightness of drifting shadow.

"Yes," she breathed as he laid her back against the seat and slid one hand underneath the high knit collar to lay a sensuous massage into the curve of her neck. His mouth caressed her cheeks and then returned to ride liquid fire into her lips.

"Do you know," he whispered, "this sweet little mouth has been haunting me. I could feel it against my skin when I closed my eyes. . . ." Warm sharpening strokes parted her lips, and his tongue swept over the access to her mouth and then inward in a light tease over the uneven line of her teeth, igniting heat waves that spread like velvet shimmers inside her chest.

The fragrance of his hair, fresh and piney, was potent in her senses. His lips tasted of the night breeze and the vivid tang of winter. His hands, moving with heart-lifting candor, had begun to burn through her coat, and then they returned to cradle her head, dragging her into his kiss, his ardent breath coming with thrilling rapidity against the damp tissues of her mouth. His palms brushed the underside of her chin and gently, carefully, spread open her coat. Her temperature fluctuated, flooding her veins with shuddering heat.

"Are you cold, Jenny?" he murmured, his tongue rimming her earlobe, his hands on her waist pressing her into him. "Let my body keep you warm. Jenny, darling Jenny." His whisper teased the inside of her ear. "Are you uncomfortable now?"

His hands wove gentle up-and-down patterns on the sides of her body, tracing her shape through her smooth sweater, caressing her ribs, the flatness of her stomach, and her rounded hips, molding her softness with exquisite sensitivity.

"Yes . . ." she breathed as his fingertips skimmed the underside of her breasts, and as his fingers gently covered her tenderness, driving the aching need deep within her, "yes . . . yes . . ."

His laughter came quietly against her cheeks, then her lips, and she drew a hard concussive breath when his fingers, wending downward, began to feed thick dreamy pleasure to the inside of her thighs. "Darling, if you're still uncomfortable" —his lips sought and nuzzled hers, showing her the outline of his smile—"I think we could find the cure."

Four

His words brought her chin up, which hardly surprised him, and her wide-set eyes gazed up at him with dismay. For a moment, she was painfully open, her unguarded sensitivity carrying the simplicity of a line drawing—Tweetybird in a tough predicament. He knew suddenly why she had grown up to be so cautious. Jennifer Hamilton was very vulnerable.

He enfolded her in his arms, watching the top of her head as her face sought the false refuge of his chest. Her fingers clung to the sides of his coat and he heard her make a soft sound, something less than a word, more than a sigh.

He knew surrender when he saw it in a woman. This was something else. Numb shock, probably. He had a sudden unsettling vision of himself as a predator—the puma holding a small struggling creature under one paw. The thought disturbed him enough to bring discipline to the fire in his senses.

The riveting sweetness of caressing her mouth with his tongue had taken him off guard. This was new to him, this overpowering need to be with a woman. The one thing he was not capable of doing right now was letting her leave his life. It was ironic that after all this time and all he'd experienced, the feeling should come in the arms of this tender, unripe person. This wasn't the way he'd expected it to happen.

He put his hand against the back of her head, stroking the sleek healthy strands of her hair, watching its subdued sheen glow like jet in the starlight. God, he thought, please don't let me hurt this woman. He knew that if he pushed deftly enough in the right direction, he could probably have her with him tonight. That knowledge brought him nothing but a weary self-accusation. A fast, easy, efficient seduction would wound her no matter how much it met the demands of his body. For her, he had to relearn intimacy.

When he felt her trying to withdraw from his arms, he let his grip slacken immediately and watched in sympathy, touched with desire and tender amusement, as she slid a little distance down the seat, straightening her shoulders with a visible attempt at dignity.

Staring with some intensity out the windshield at the frozen, twisted line of trees across the field, she slowly drew off her mitten and touched bare unsteady fingertips to her damp lips. Her hand dropped. She cleared her throat. "You're very thorough."

Admiring the pluckiness that made her continue to resist him, he said, "Which, I take it, is not a characteristic you find endearing?"

"People who are good at everything depress me."

"Don't worry. I have moments of great ineptitude."

Glaring blankly out the window, she said, "I have *hours* of great ineptitude."

He wanted to take her in his arms again but he couldn't, because the desire to make love to her was still stinging his body. Instead, he rested his arm on the seat back, his fingertips stroking her shoulder, running along the pliant groove of her jacket seam. Then, without wanting it to happen, his fingers strayed to her face, tracing the line of her nose, the gently rounded nostrils, the entrancing corner of her lips. I want you, he thought. I want you, lady.

He slid his fingers underneath her soft knit cap to explore the warm hollows of her ear. "D'you know something?"

"What?"

The slight breathless quality in her voice found a strong answering vibration within his body that took a heavier struggle than he had anticipated to subdue. The face she turned toward him, though wary, seemed to have no idea what effect she had on his body chemistry. He grinned inwardly. It wasn't safe to allow this poor kid out after dark!

He withdrew his hand and started the engine. "You don't really cringe."

Jennifer, watching the skillful, intriguing motions of his hands on the steering wheel, was trying to fathom how Philip Brooks had happened to a life that until now had been droning along at a pleasantly mundane rate.

It had begun to snow, gay tumbling drops that grew bright in the headlights, scattering like breeze-blown blossoms. Black and dramatic, the

naked tree limbs met in tangled embraces overhead. Behind the stars, the sky was the color of
magic.

Magic. When they reached the turnoff that would
have permitted them to double back toward the
Victorian Arms, the car swept onward. Jennifer
closed her eyes. *I hope he's kidnapping me.* Abandoned to the wolves . . . She was forced to begin
redefining the wolf. Unexpected depths had surfaced in a man she had expected to be shallow. He
was funny, forceful, and clever. If it was difficult
to tell whether he was kind or merely charming, it
didn't seem to lessen his appeal. She spent a
moment thinking about the word "appeal." To say
that Philip Brooks had appeal was to win a black
belt in understatement.

Philip Brooks. The name caught and held in
her mind, printing and reprinting. Brooks had a
special meaning in Wisconsin, as Rockefeller had
in other parts of the country. One studied it in
elementary school history classes. A grand and
eclectic family, they had made a fortune in banking and put it into consolidating small railroad
companies throughout the Midwest. Outstanding
philanthropists, their names showered the pedi-
ments of art centers and libraries all over the
state. She had a flashing memory of the M.C. at
the Cougar Club introducing Philip as a "native
blueblood" which she had paid no attention to at
the time. And there was the patrician accent—
never explained. Surely it was impossible for a
true Brooks, precious to the state's historical
heritage, to be peeling off his jeans in a raucous
nightclub. The thought shocked her more than any
other thing that had occurred this strange evening.

The station wagon stopped in front of a mammoth gateway, the tall brickwork and wrought iron bristling with rank and importance. It was the portal to the Brooks estate.

Philip depressed a disk on a small control that sat on the dashboard and the gate swung apart as though it had been whisked open by invisible hands. Jennifer thought immediately of the magical palace in *Beauty and the Beast.* The beast's palace. The outrageous but not unappealing idea that Philip was going to take her to a cozy bachelor pad and make love to her gave way to a truly terrifying notion: not only might he be sinfully wealthy, he might also be taking her to a far from cozy mansion to introduce her to his parents. He wouldn't. He couldn't.

"I hope that I don't seem vulgarly inquisitive," she said in a voice that was distinct and polite. "But where are we going?"

"I'd like to make you acquainted with some friends of mine."

Friends. "Do they live in a mansion?"

"No." His smile enlarged the word. "In trees."

That set her back. The wagon traversed fifty yards of a wooded drive and then turned bumpily into a narrow, snow-packed lane. Stiff branches pelted the car doors and windows with a clapping rattle. High withered grass reached through the snow to brush the car frame. She wondered if there was some inoffensive manner of phrasing a question that asked teasingly if these mysterious tree dwelling friends were members of the ape family. She had decided there was not when he said, "You don't wear perfume," as though it had just occurred to him.

For some odd reason there was approval in his voice. "True. I never remember."

"That's good. They might not have liked it."

They live in trees. They don't like perfume. Hokay. The ultraconservatism of someone who could be offended by women wearing perfume accorded not at all with someone leading a raffish and precarious existence in a tree house. The man was pulling her leg.

"These friends of yours—they *are* human?"

"Jennifer! I strip. Would I expose you to any of my unsavory associates?" he asked playfully.

His tone was light as spun sugar, amusement rimmed the corners of the long fascinating mouth, and yet some little understood sense within her seemed to be registering his subtle anxiety. Or it might have been her imagination. Surely it wasn't possible that this beautiful, bossy, sensual person could be that vulnerable.

Anyway, every shred of evidence indicated that he came from a family whose members shipped their money to the bank in semitrailers. One wouldn't think he had to work at all, much less at something that disturbed him. Confused as she was, she couldn't bring herself to ask him about his family directly. His connection or at least what seemed to be his connection to wealth and power was strangely embarrassing to her. She wasn't sure why, perhaps because it seemed so alien. Reared herself in a genteel, modest prosperity in the milieu of the small college where her mother had taught economics, she had experienced nothing of the world of the great and grand beyond the fairy tale version of it depicted on television and

in films. But surely these people didn't let their
sons strip in nightclubs.

"Why do you do it?" she asked, her voice raised
to carry over the scratching branches. Studying
his face intently in the reflected gleam of the headlights she caught every nuance of his expression
as it became a powerful combination of cynical
amusement and some darker thing that she barely
glimpsed.

Tersely he said, "They pay me." He paused. "A
lot."

She might have pointed out that there were
plenty of other jobs that would have done the
same without requiring him to take off his clothes.
But the memory of his kiss was growing warmer
inside her instead of fading, and the sky was the
color of magic. Jennifer relaxed back into the seat—
and into the new and wonderful glow of frivolity.

"More than the Emerald Lake Library, do you
think?" she asked. "Can women be Cougars too?
Do you give lessons?"

"Yes. No. And I'd be delighted to show you how
to take off your clothes. To be honest, though,
I'd be much more interested in results than in
technique."

I asked for that, she thought. How interesting
of me. I wish—oh, dear Lord, *how I wish*—he
would stop this car and kiss me again.

The car did stop soon. He killed the engine in a
small clearing and turned to her in the darkness.

"Now we have to wait."

"What for?"

"Our eyes need to adjust to the night. Do you
know much about night vision?"

"No." She was beginning to find Philip Brooks

more and more fascinating. "Except that it's an excuse to make kids eat carrots."

"Yes. Because deficiency in vitamin A can impair night vision. The retina of your eye is covered with rod cells and cone cells. The rods are sensitive to light. The cones are sensitive to color and they can't function very efficiently in dim light. That's why you can't see colors in the dark." He slipped an arm around her shoulders and drew her to his sturdy comfort. "Look at the sky."

Jennifer looked at the sky and thought about how close his sensitive fingers were to her breast.

"That black velvet sky is just as blue now as it was in the day," he said. "Our eyes don't work well enough to see it. But they can still do much better than most people realize. There's a chemical in the rod cells of the retina that decomposes as it reacts to light, but in dim light, you can synthesize it faster than light can break it down so you build up a good supply. Once your eyes are fully dark-adapted they become many times more light sensitive than in bright light. Hmm." He tilted up her chin on a strong finger and examined her face. "You must have a higher threshold of boredom than most of my friends. You're still awake! And," he continued softly, "you've begun to smile, miracle of miracles." His thumb was tracing the upcurve of her lips as they tipped to meet the slow descent of his.

She heard him breathe, "Don't stop," just before the sparklingly sweet meeting of their lips. It felt good to her, so good, as his mouth moved against the tautness of her smile. Gently, he stroked her tingling flesh with his lower lip and then brought his mouth into light contact with hers, rocking against her mouth, parting her. His hand skimmed up her back to the base of her neck in a light, tantalizing massage before it swept slowly down to cover her breast. The pressure of fabric and of his steady fingers pushed heavy flutters of sensation through her chest and her skin responded to each nuance of his cupping palm. Some impulse of the night's magic made her bring her arms up and clasp them around his neck, and lean into his body. One of his hands moved to accommodate her, pressing her close; and the other continued its lazily kindling motion against her coat and the flushing softness beneath.

"How long does it take"—she drew in a shaking gulp of air as his thumb discovered her nipple— "for this thing to happen to our eyes."

"In thirty minutes we'll be doing very well. In the meantime, tell me how you spent your day." His voice sounded slightly breathless as he nestled her against his jacket.

She protested with a startled, uncertain laugh that *nobody's* boredom threshold was high enough for that.

Smiling, he began to ask her questions. What time did she get up in the morning? Was getting up hard or easy for her? What did she eat for breakfast? Did she listen to music or was her house quiet? What did she sleep in? Some of the questions teased; others tititlated. Some were serious and she began to find herself following the mood of them, explaining the flow of her day, her job, her thoughts, the people she saw and worked with. Never before had anyone explored her life in such lively detail. No one had cared before that she liked apple jelly and beds with fishnet lace canopies, or that she was making a Shaker chair from a kit in her spare time or that she stopped every morning on the way to work at Lake Park to feed the uneaten half of her English muffin to the mallards. No one but her mother had asked about the intricacies of settling into a new job and establishing oneself with a talented and experienced staff.

Not many minutes ago she had accused him of being thorough, and he was. He was probably the most thorough, observant listener she had ever conversed with. She stopped watching to learn whether or not this was only the élan of some surface charm. She forgot to worry.

His hands explored her with the same sympathetic seductiveness as his voice, which had become husky, a murmur. Time passed, a flowing gift. Her eyes became dark-adjusted. Her body became love-adjusted.

"I think you're ready now," he said softly.

She jumped.

Laughing gently at her belated alarm, he slid down the zipper of her coat, drew it down from her shoulders and then zipped her into his own parka. His warm sweet scent rose from the down lining, enveloping her as she watched him pull a wool melton jacket from the back seat and shrug into it. He climbed out of the car and held open her door invitingly.

She knew the hours that followed would live in her memory forever. The forest was a jeweled world. Snowflakes glittered from clumps of puffy snow caught on pine branches. The ground twinkled as if it were strewn with chipped stars. Night breezes lulled the high scalloped tree crowns and cast the incense of damp cedar into the moist, snow-spangled air.

She could pick out detail in the moonlight as if it were day. As she turned slowly, looking around her in the dazzling silence, Philip took buckets from the back of the car and filled them with kibble-style dog food. He handed her a stack of tin pie plates and began to walk with her toward an opening in the forest wall, their footsteps muffled in the dense snow carpet. She no longer noticed the cold.

"Where—"

A softly spoken word interrupted her. "Whisper."

"Where are we going?" Her low tone mated with his. "Do you have a kennel here?"

"No." He smiled. "I have wild friends."

Beyond, a meadow bathed in starlight. She watched Philip fill the pie plates and put them on the ground. Then he took her face in his hands and kissed her once, slowly, and she tasted the mist of his breath and snowflakes.

Like a dreamer she walked hand-in-hand with him to the meadow's edge where he took her in his arms under the drooping canopy of a willow. Amid the ice droplets that glistened like tear-shaped gems at the tip of each branch, he caressed the snowflakes from her lashes with his lips. Then, gently, he turned her back toward the meadow, and stood close behind her, his hands spanning her waist to hold her comfortably.

His hushed whisper caressed her ear. "It's better not to stand behind a tree when you watch animals in the wild. Otherwise, you'll have to move to peer around the tree and animals find movement threatening. When you stand perfectly still, in the shadow of a tree, you become almost invisible. If you have to move, do it very slowly, and if you accidentally make a noise, freeze. Also, try not to stare head-on. Predators stare directly at their prey when they're sizing it up for attack, so for most animals staring has bad associations."

He didn't speak again, nor did she.

The meadow was alive. Her heart beat slowly, like the delicate and deliberate footsteps of the three does that came to drink from a spring-fed stream.

Raccoons emerged, masked bandits from the darkness. Trundling toward the pie plates with heads low, backs humped up, chittering to each other, they reminded Jennifer of the early crowd at a diner. They ate methodically, their paws working like little black hands. Some dipped the kibble in the stream, leaving the bank a smeary mess. Plentiful as the food was, once or twice there was some greediness and a spat broke out. It was hard not to laugh out loud at the indignant tremble of whiskers and upturned black noses. A skunk ambled out from a sway of grasses and took his place at the pie plates as though it were a cafeteria. She laughed again, softly, as the other diners withdrew to a disgruntled distance. Philip's voice, soft as the harp-song of the breeze in the pines, began to tell her about the animals; about the amiable little skunk who couldn't seem to understand why everyone avoided her, about the raccoons and how many seasons he had known them. Later he told her about the red fox that stole with alert concern across the meadow and the great horned owl that flew above the trees with the silence of a spirit. The winter night opened as a fresh universe, warm with personality and purity.

As the moon peered at them over the stark tree limbs, she watched muskrats take vegetable scraps from Philip's hands. A porcupine lumbered up to him eagerly and he fed salt to it.

Sitting on the wagon's tailgate, she drank coffee from his thermos, a red plaid wool blanket spread over her lap. She gazed in new wonder at the snowflakes he caught on his jacket and showed her through a small illuminated magnifying lens. Each separate crystal carried its own special beauty.

She was enraptured.

The same gentle hands that had given her his stillness under the willow laid her back on the wagon bed, stroking her cheeks, parting the zipper of her parka and his jacket to bring their bodies together. He held her, just held her, rubbing his body slowly against hers to warm her chilled flesh, and told her about the legends of the night, the forest; and about the spring that soon would come and the animal young that would fill the trees and streams.

And she was enraptured.

He returned her to her doorstep in the dewy mantle of a setting moon. Then and only then did he kiss her again, gathering her to him with heart-lifting care, bringing his mouth to hers, holding her in a deep, steady kiss that they both broke from breathing quickly and hard. For a long, helpless moment she met his wantonly beautiful gaze. Then he touched her forehead lightly with a graceful finger, whispered, "Sleep well," and left her.

Five

Habits die hard. By morning, Jennifer began to worry.

The reassurance of his presence might have helped, but by midweek he had not tried to see her. And that brought home the torments a relationship with a man like Philip Brooks would cause. He was not a stranger to her, and never would be again, and yet she had no way to know if he hadn't called because he was busy, or indifferent, or complacent. Or if in that one night together he had satisfied whatever instinct had impelled him to pursue her. This wasn't going to be simple.

By the end of the week, two things had happened that made it seem impossible.

The first was a letter from her mother that arrived Wednesday.

My daughter—my refined, public-television addict of a daughter—at a strip show? I'm aghast!

I'm horrified. I'm coming down on the next bus to see it too. No, that was a joke, but I really may come sometime. A group of women from my office is talking about spending the weekend at the Maple Lodge near Emerald Lake, on their lovely cross-country ski trails, before the snow goes back up to heaven. Believe it or not, we might come on Friday night to see the show at the Cougar Club first. The others, young things in their thirties, are getting a big kick out of the idea of trying to corrupt me, and you know what? Just once before I die, I'd like the chance to leer at a man. After forty-one years in a sexist world, I have it coming. By the way, I *have* seen the most beautiful man in the world. My secretary was down at the Cougar Club last month, and brought back a Polaroid of their star. Which was the thing that got everyone here so set on coming. When I read your letter, I thought yes, the young Alexander. What a waste, when you think of it, someone with a face full of character like that. You'd think he could have done anything with his life. That aside, I think you should have kissed him.

The second incident occurred on Thursday afternoon when Jennifer almost walked into the staff room in search of the *Publisher's Weekly* that Annette had carried off earlier. It was Annette's voice sweeping around the slightly open door that froze Jennifer on the threshold.

". . . that Jennifer was dating Philip Brooks? You could have knocked me over with an index card when Eleanor came out with it"—fingers snapped briskly—"just like that."

"You're the last soul in town to find out, then." The second voice belonged to Lydia's younger sister Tracy, a high-school senior earning extra credit by helping part time in the library. "Mr. Caras was out plowing snow in the storm last weekend and he saw Philip bringing her home in the wee hours. He said it was quite a goodnight kiss they had too. Ooo-la-*la*. He practically ran the old plow into the ditch."

"Too bad he didn't." It was Lydia's voice, the tone caustic. "The old poop. I can't tell you how sorry I feel for Philip Brooks. He can't sneeze without half the county betting on whether he's going to whip out a hanky or a tissue."

"Oh, I don't know about that," Annette said wryly. "Eleanor still doesn't realize he's dancing at the Cougar Club."

"Who'd dare to tell her? She'd die. You know how the old guard feels about that family. The Brooks name equals royalty."

"True enough," Annette answered. A pause filled with the trickle of pouring coffee. "Jennifer is about the last person in the world I expected to see next on the Brooks menu. He doesn't usually go in for—"

"Cold cuts." A chuckle from Tracy.

"That was mean." There was a frown in Lydia's voice.

"And not what I meant," Annette said coolly. "She may seem a little reserved sometimes but she's actually a very warm person. You should see her with the children."

"Like the Pied Piper," Lydia agreed around a swallow of coffee.

"She's wonderful. Pretty, too. Exquisite really, and I don't think she has any idea. She's so unassuming about herself. What I was going to say was that he usually doesn't make a meal of someone who's obviously tender." A lighter snapped. A whiff of cigarette smoke wafted through the doorway. "Where on earth do you think she could have met him?" The silence seemed to shrug. "I know she couldn't have met him before we took her to the Cougar Club. I mean, she surely would have said something, right? Listen, this is one sophisticated guy. Do you think we ought to warn her that the man has what understatement would call—a certain notoriety for letting almost no one into his life?"

"Ugh. Interference!" said Lydia. "Still—"

"You two are crazy!" Tracy sounded indignant. "If Philip Brooks asked either one of you out, you sure as heck wouldn't be listening to a lot of cautious advice from your friends. Ten minutes of Philip Brooks is better than no minutes of Philip Brooks. Notorious, my foot. Who cares? He's awesome."

Silence. "The kid's right," Annette said.

Tracy chuckled suddenly.

"What?"

"The kid knows something you don't know," Tracy's voice teased.

"What?" Annette said. "By gum, Lydia, look at how sly she looks. All right, young'un, tell."

A quick pause. Then, with significance, Tracy's voice. "He's July."

"Who? What are you talking about?"

"Philip Brooks. You know. In your calendar." Another chuckle. "You mean you haven't even looked in your own calendar? I *thought* you just got it to bug Eleanor. Philip Brooks is July."

"Are you kidding?" There was a short flurry of movement. Pages ruffled wildly. A silence. A burst of excited laughter, stifled painfully.

"Lordy, lordy. Will you look at that? She speaks no less than the truth. The man is July." Annette's voice sounded strange. "The man is July and I want him so much it makes my stomach hurt. What he does to my insides ought to be illegal."

"He's an aphrodisiac on legs." Lydia laughed. "Hey, cut it out, Trace. You're getting fingerprints on his thigh."

Jennifer was five feet away before she knew she was stepping backward. The children's section was a safe haven, where she scooped up somebody small in a quilted crawler, found a large book, and took both with her into the depths of a beanbag chair to read aloud, hiding her face and her scathing embarrassment behind the friendly pages.

That night brought her new restlessness, new unease. She tried to see herself clearly, with her strengths and weaknesses. She was romantic, amiable like the little skunk unless threatened, and filled with a thousand picture dreams of how the world ought to be . . . and only rarely was. Some of the most enchanting hours of her life had been spent in Philip's forest, but any relationship she had with him would have to be lived in the real world. And it would take a certain toughness, a certain quality of imperviousness that she would have to develop for the fleeting span of

Philip's interest. Nor was she composed emotionally for the heady lightning of short spectacular love affairs. She needed things around her that grew and lasted. She needed security.

About the man himself, she tried not to think at all; not about the breathtaking physical countenance, the deft gentle hands, the generous mouth. Nor the engaging manner, nor the mystery of why anyone with his background had come to be July.

She shed tears and faced the truth that Philip Brooks and Jennifer Hamilton were not meant to work.

The glow of his remembered presence stayed with her, and their winter night together slept uneasily at the edge of her conscious thoughts. It hardly helped that the preschool story hour she had planned for Friday had the topic of "Animals."

At two o'clock on Friday afternoon, the three- and four-year-olds came tumbling into the children's section. Working hard to learn names, and smiling into little faces, she showed the thirty tots magazines with brightly colored animal pictures, a film strip about how puppies grew, and read aloud from books of animal stories. She admired and displayed on the bulletin board their crayon drawings and snapshots of their pets. She taught them the eensy-weensy-spider finger play. And rolling up the cuffs of her puff-sleeved pink striped blouse, hitching her pleated pants, she got right down on the carpet with them and became animals. They were elephants, swinging their arms for trunks, squirting themselves with water. They were bunnies, sitting up on their haunches, wriggling their noses to sniff for carrots, hopping through the grass. New animals entered her repertoire too: a waddling porcupine, and raccoons that ate with tiny dexterous fingers, and deer shaking snow-flakes from their tails.

Jennifer was a monkey, squatting on the floor beside a little girl in braids and a Smurf shirt, peeling an imaginary banana, making monkey noises through an outthrust simian jaw. When she curved a hand upward over her head to scratch lazily at an armpit, the sweep of her gaze caught a freeze-frame filled with Philip Brooks. He was standing twenty feet away, watching her, a slim hip in softly-stretched denim resting against a low case of encyclopedias.

Fate, do you have it in for me?

The need to maintain her slipping grasp on the precipice of sanity would not permit her to look back but she retained the impression of porcelain blue eyes, sensitive lips uptilted in amusement, an open down jacket, a shapely hand curved around a pair of cashmere gloves. She had the dreadful feeling that her skin was turning chalk white, but without missing a beat, she smacked her lips to finish the last of her pretend banana, offering the final bite to her little friend in the pigtails, who chewed solemnly.

In front of a sea of trusting faces and Philip Brooks, she did her final animal, a seal, showing the interested audience how to squirm across the floor on forearms that were flippers, dragging their lower body behind. She and thirty preschoolers barked and balanced balls on their noses.

Getting stiffly to her feet, walking around helping out little seals, she asked cheerfully, "How many of you have met Jinx, our new gerbil? I'm going to bring him out so that you can say 'hello.' "

Lydia, who had been helping her, was waiting with a very peculiar expression on her face beside the low pine table that held the refurbished aquarium where Jinx lived. Under her breath, out of the corner of her mouth like a B-movie mobster, she muttered, "Philip is here."

"I saw him." Elaborately calm, Jennifer removed the wire cage cover. "Maybe he wants to check out a book."

"Hum. You must not have noticed the way he's watching you. He wants to check out a librarian. I'll take the rest of the hour. You go talk to him. If he stands around much longer like that, one of us may go and attack him. We're only human. Oh, my Lord, you aren't really intending to pick that . . . that *thing* up, are you?"

"Yes." Jinx dove under a pile of bedding as Jennifer tried awkwardly to scoop him up. "It's important for me to show no fear. Positive early experiences with animals are essential to a child's development of—" She broke off, and said *sotto voce* into the cage, "Quit the funny business, you furry little fink, or I'll trade you in on a hamster."

Lydia laughed surreptitiously. "I don't see how you can touch it. It looks like a—"

"I know what it looks like," Jennifer said grimly, lifting Jinx. "If Mr. Greenjeans can do it, I can do it." Turning to her innocent audience, she tried to let nothing show in her face except warm delight in and tolerance for the unique varieties of animal life on the green earth. "Jinx is a lot like a mouse. In fact, he comes from the same family," she exclaimed enthusiastically, as if that were a great thing. She loved animals; studying and watching them had always seemed to her one of the chief pleasures in life, but she knew her strong feelings had the dewy-eyed sentimentality of a Bambi-syndrome dilettante. When it came to practical experience, she had virtually none.

"You may come up one at a time and say hello to him by petting him very carefully with one finger." She stroked his back with her forefinger to illustrate. Jinx, meanwhile, had stepped experimentally out onto her wrist with the cautious air of someone testing a rickety foot bridge. A knee-high towhead with jam on his mouth ran up.

"Me first! Me first!" he said, poking an inquisitive finger into Jinx's face. Jinx, deciding that discretion was the better part of valor, skittered into Jennifer's sleeve and up her arm without looking backward, dashed across the no-man's land of her chest to her other shoulder, his little body making a wiggly hump before it plunged down her back.

The children loved it, and in any other circumstances she would have delighted in their tinkling splashes of laughter. But Jinx had tiny sharp little claws, and her tucked blouse prevented his egress. He lost patience, poking his tickling nose, wiggling his body, searching for a foothold at the base of her spine.

Smiling weakly, with shivers skittering up and down her back, she said, "Silly Jinx. Do you see that, boys and girls? Jinx is playing with Miss Jennifer." Then, the B-movie mobster aside to Lydia: "Please. Get him out!"

"Oh no. No way. I feel for you, believe me, but one touch of that glorified mouse and I'm likely to pass out. Untuck your blouse and shake him out."

"I couldn't! Poor little guy, he might get hurt." Not only the potential fall but an excited stampede of plastic snowbooted feet could be highly dangerous to Jinx's future.

"For heaven's sake then, slip into the staff room and get Eleanor to help you," Lydia hissed with a grin. "I'll read the kids a couple of story books. Scoot!"

Because it was well nigh impossible to maintain any dignity when the person inside the poised facade was mentally hopping around the room shrieking "eeek," she gave the laughing children a sickly grin. She told them she'd be back soon and beat a hasty retreat toward the staff door. But the commotion had drawn Eleanor, who was looking on in a rather aghast way from the encyclopedia case where, Jennifer was alarmed to see, Philip Brooks was still comfortably established.

"Hello, Philip," she said, a little breathlessly, and directed a pleading look at Eleanor in passing. "Eleanor, if I could borrow you for a moment or two in the staff room . . ."

Assuming that Eleanor would follow her directly, she fled to the staff room with Jinx digging at the waistband of her slacks. Waiting alone in the small room, she rested her hands against the paper-jumbled desk, closing her eyes and pulling in a long restorative breath. Her heart was engaging in the maniacal syncopation that she had come to know as the Philip Brooks rhythm.

Behind her, the staff room door closed.

"Eleanor, *thank* you. Please hurry. I think he's chewing on the elastic of my underpants—"

A gentle suggestive finger found the slight hollow behind her neck and traced slowly downward.

There was no mistaking her body's response to that touch.

"Philip—" she whispered.

"There's no understanding it, but Eleanor didn't seem especially thrilled with the idea of plucking up Jinx from his travels. It wasn't very difficult to convince her to yield the floor to a specialist," he said.

Firm hands turned her body, and she found herself staring up into smiling light-filled eyes.

"Poor Miss Jennifer's in a fix," he murmured, his fingers slipping down her body until they reached the first button of her blouse, the base of his palms barely brushing the upper rise of her breasts, and she felt a soft puff of sensual awareness spreading in her chest. His lips touched hers briefly and the top button of her blouse slipped open.

For a moment, her desire to press herself fully into his embrace overcame her, but whiskers tickled her back and her ill-functioning sense of self-preservation reared its abashed head enough to bring her to her senses. Drawing away, fumbling to pull her blouse closed, she gasped out, "Jinx is in back."

"I know." His dark brows lifted innocently. The long mouth quirked. "But how can I get my hand underneath your shirt if it's buttoned so tightly? Sit down." He pressed her gently onto the edge of the desk chair. "Don't worry. I'll fish out Jinx for you. Relax and rest your worried head against my—" He glanced down teasingly as though he were estimating which part of his anatomy her head would fall against. "Let's call it my stomach."

He could call it anything he wanted, but if she

laid her cheek sideways, it would *not* have been against his stomach. Her upper body seemed to shock into a new state of wakefulness as his fingers twisted under her collar, following the curve of her back downward.

"When I came in, I never guessed I'd have this charming opportunity to grope under your—Hold still! I won't be responsible for the consequences if he runs around in front and decides to snuggle up against the warmth of your—" Dissolving into laughter at her reaction, "No, no. Hush now, darling. Don't try to get up. I've almost got him. There!"

Her shoulders trembled under the flood of receding tension as his graceful thighs moved backward a step and his hand moved up and out of her shirt.

She watched Philip carry Jinx toward his face on an upturned palm, churring softly to the tiny gerbil. Jinx stretched up on tiptoe to peer alertly into Philip's eyes, sniffing with affection and then with ravenous interest as Philip produced a sunflower seed from his pocket.

Philip smiled as the gerbil took the seed in its forepaws and deftly slit the shell. Studying Jinx while he munched, he said, "You really know how to liven up a story hour. Why'd you decide to become a librarian?"

Shaking herself out of her amazement that he just happened to have a pocketful of Jinx's favorite treat, she began to close her blouse with fingers that trembled. "When I was eight years old, I was carrying a stack of books to the checkout desk in my public library and a boy pushed me from behind as a joke. When I dropped my books on the floor, one of the librarians shushed me angrily. It was very traumatic because I was a quiet child and no one had ever scolded me in public. I decided that when I grew up I'd have a library too, but my library would never be like hers."

His eyes strayed briefly, thoughtfully, to hers before he emptied the few papers from the wicker waste basket and lowered Jinx inside with a scattering of sunflower seeds. Downy-light as the touch of his eyes had been, she felt entered, analyzed, absorbed. . . . Without the gerbil in his hand, he looked much more dangerous. Trying to cloak her inner desperation, she sped on, "Everyone said they'd graduate me with a bun on the back of my head and a pencil stuck in it but as you can see, I've cut my hair and . . ."

His fingers in her hair, penetrating to her scalp, running along the edge of her ear brought her words to a warbling halt.

"I like your hair short," he murmured, dropping a soft kiss on the curve of her throat. "It's cute. And you have a lovely neck."

An easy motion of his hand brought a chair in front of hers and he sat down facing her, his body very close, one of his knees separating hers. Her breath caught at the sudden pleasure-filled uplift in her abdomen from the pressure of his leg inside her thigh. Her gaze dropped involuntarily to his legs. There was a mesmeric fascination in the way his lean muscles tugged at the age-polished denim, and she found herself following the taut line upward with her eyes until it occurred to her what she was doing. Her cheeks were flooding with color as she tried to pretend that she had

only been trying to study the logo on his faded
sweatshirt. She recognized the famous alien there
with a jolt.

"E.T.?", she asked suddenly.

"Yes. Shall I show you how to turn on my heart
light?"

Her gaze flew to his and held there suspended
in the perception and tenderness and dancing
light she saw in his eyes.

Giving her a little grin, he began to walk two
fingers up her thigh, murmuring, "Eensy weensy
spider . . ."

Seeing that she was continuing to stare at
him in the transfixed way he was not unaccus-
tomed to receiving from women, he tried again.
"There's no telling what Jinx might have been up
to under your shirt. You'd better let me check
your underwear."

Her deepening flush and steady wide-eyed gaze,
the engaging rise and fall of her breasts against
the light fabric of her blouse, the dusky barely
parted lips, were drawing deep-rooted answers from
his senses; and his desire to have his arms filled
with her became almost as great as his desire to
make her smile. Holding her waist in a light clasp,
he drew her toward him, setting her on his leg
with her thighs straddling one of his. What the
pressure of her delicately hugging thighs aroused
in him showed in his voice as he murmured, "You
make a ravishing monkey." One of his palms
slipped upward to massage her neck, bringing
her lips slowly toward his. "Want to monkey
around?"

But her warm unsteady fingers covered his
mouth gently, a stubborn mute barrier. Her other

hand pressed shakily against his chest, begging for space.

"Philip, no."

Under his hands he could feel the tense hold of her body, the winsome trembling in her thighs. He could sense her lacerating inner struggle against the violent flame that was the mirror of his own. He searched her expressive brown eyes.

"No?" he asked.

"No." She whispered the word and tried to slide away, her warm inner thighs brushing over his jeans. His hands stopped her.

"Why?"

"Because—Philip, please. Let me go. I can't think with my—with your leg in between . . ."

He released her and watched her go to stand against the desk, closing her eyes, catching the edge in a pale-knuckled grip. It struck him then that she was saying no to more than the kiss. She was saying no to everything. There was an odd despair in her face and he echoed that as he had her desire. In a lifetime of hearing yes, the first shy, sane voice to break the babble that his life had become was telling him no. Don't you want to be my redemption? he thought. He tried to choose what he would feel, to corral and control and confront it, but the emotions were too new, too unfamiliar.

She watched him stand, glance around the room in a distracted restless fashion, and then absently lift a nearly empty roll of paper towels from an upper shelf. He removed the last paper sheets, and selecting scissors from the pencil can, cut the cardboard roll in half. For a bewildered moment, she had no idea what he was doing. Then she saw him set the cardboard rolls in the wicker basket. After a cautious minute, the gerbil came to sniff at them, and then darted inside one. Philip had made a toy for Jinx. It was a small thing, but it touched her. Her throat grew uncomfortably tight as he sat back down facing her, his dramatic, endless legs stretched out with the wine-colored boots crossed at the ankle, the shapeless cling of the sweatshirt outlining the hard modeling of his upper body. He met her eyes and repeated, "Why?"

The subtle tracing of feeling she had seen earlier on his face seemed to have vanished and she began to wonder if it had been there at all. The blue eyes were only clear and curious, the long mouth relaxed. She had never felt less articulate.

"It would be too complicated," she said.

His head tilted slightly. His eyes affected interest. "Is that based in something concrete or is this more of the 'I don't trust men because they're strange and have body parts that change size' doctrine?"

"If you think I'm that ridiculous, it's a wonder I intrigue you at all."

That drew a smile. "When you're ridiculous, you're wonderful. We only begin to have problems when you try to be consistent."

He stuffed his hands into the pockets of his jeans, the action unconsciously drawing her tense attention back to the taut pull of fabric over his hip bones. Pummeling herself mentally, she watched him stand once more—the restlessness again, what did it mean? He gave Jinx another sunflower seed. His gaze strayed around the room. It lit softly, suddenly, on the Cougar Club calendar and the contraction in her throat spread downward to her stomach when he reached out one patrician hand to flip the pages open to July. Dispassionately, he surveyed the beautiful nude photograph of himself.

"It's because I strip, isn't it?" He looked up at her and gave her a smile of heart-stopping charm. "Don't think another thing about it. I'm sure everyone who comes to the show is only interested in my mind."

She turned away, fighting to enforce the slipping hold on her will. He came to her and caught hold of her shoulders, bringing her to him. She sensed something in him that reminded her queerly of exhaustion as he laid his forehead against hers, his fingers gently kneading through her thin blouse.

"Jenny, Jenny . . . Why do you have to make this a problem?" he whispered. He must have felt her resistance, her fierce hold to decisions made in cooler moments, because he raised his head, looking down into her worried eyes, his hands resting loosely on her shoulders.

"All right then. Let's explore your consistencies," he said. "If I posed nude as an artist's model would that disturb you?"

Knowing that she was going for a baited hook, yet not able to resist the temptation, she said, "I'm not sure. Probably not as much."

"I see. You like a high culture tag on your exposed skin. What if I was an artist who painted nudes?"

She was becoming blindingly conscious of his thumbs, which were making leisured uplifting circles under her collarbone. "That would be different."

"High culture," he repeated dryly, "and you prefer the exploiter to the exploited. Smart."

"Now just a—"

"What if I were a doctor and spent the day examining naked bodies?"

Exasperated, and yet enchanted by him, she said, "Doctors at least don't kiss their patients."

"True. But maybe they should. Kissing someone for a buck is significantly more wholesome and probably more therapeutic than sticking your fingers into their body cavities for fifty dollars an hour. Oh no!" He shortcut her sudden effort to jerk herself out of his grip. "There's one more thing I want to know, love." His next words, an urgent whisper, formed themselves against her mouth. "How does this fit into your logic?"

Logic evaporated like steam as his mouth moved in a soft eddy over hers, dragging her lips into fragile openness. His knee rubbed over her outer thigh as it flexed just enough to permit his hand to slide over her back and lower, his slowly rotating palm lifting her into the hard cradle of his hips. With a seizure of need, she melted forward into the firm welcoming frame, her restive senses seeking him, learning his pliant flesh, the complex detail of projecting bone structure, the sensitive strength of his hands. Her fingers found his shoulders, the sides of his face, winnowed the fawn-soft delicacy of his hair. Each part of her that pressed his body stung with the tingling hunger to know more of him.

His gentle swirling kisses altered, and his hands burned their way upward to form a nest for her head as they guided her deeper into kisses and slow tongue strokes that carried the motion of physical love. He had stopped courting her defenses. This was a preliminary, the shattering avowal of a love act that was not to follow and they broke from it gasping, sex-flushed, though she saw with enhanced insight that in his experience, he could control it much more accurately than she.

His hands left her, resculpting themselves quickly to her cheekbones, his thumbs gently lifting her chin.

"When you—" He stopped, taking in a betraying breath. "When you decide to pull your head out of the sand, come see me. You know all the places to look."

Six

He left her with a hammering pulse and the image of his mouth wet-burned into hers. And she knew the moment she let him walk out the door that it was a mistake. No woman in her right mind would have let that man walk out of her life. Because Philip Brooks had won. She liked him. She desired him. More, she respected him. Staring into the wicker waste basket, watching Jinx's whiskers poking out of the end of a paper towel roll, she made an important discovery about human nature. One didn't always hand one's heart to another human being. Sometimes, it just went.

The library closed late, and she stood in the darkened back hallway wishing that he was waiting for her outside. She pulled her coat from the hook, and stopped, staring at the muffler still hanging there. For the first time that week, she admitted that she wasn't wearing it because it was the scarf her hand had happened to fall on.

She was wearing it because it was his. His, and because of that, somehow precious. She traced down the muffler's soft length with a fingertip and then brought it to her face, rubbing her cheek against it unseeingly. Philip Brooks. She had survived the good-humored teasing about his sudden appearance and much speculated upon assistance to her in the staff room that afternoon from Annette, Lydia, and Tracy. Surely that was a beginning.

Tonight was her turn to drive, and she let Eleanor off with a friendly wave, turning down a hospitable offer to join her for popcorn and an episode of Masterpiece Theatre preserved on the video recorder.

Inside she was drifting, her mind awash with the aggressive idiocy of what she was doing as she directed her old Volkswagen Beetle toward the Brooks mansion at Lily Hill. She knew only one thing. If she was going to Philip Brooks, she would have to do it quickly, before thought returned. Quickly and without thinking. Just do it, like a paratrooper making a jump into fog-saturated space.

An arctic cold front had sliced the state and the steadily dropping temperatures were keeping the prudent indoors. Traffic was light on the country roads. Across the lake, she could see the lights of the village as a distant glitter that threw fading streamers on the lake's frosty glass. Within the curtain of trees, the towering ramparts of oak and maple, there was no light except that from the headlamps, piercing far in the clear, frigid air, yet revealing little beyond smoky tunnel glimpses of road and brush. The cold seemed to burn out even light.

Her imagination flared, throwing up the disquieting fantasy that she was the last soul left on earth after a nuclear holocaust, utterly alone. Alone forever. She swallowed hard and turned on the radio for company, and heard the weather reporter announce with an eloquent shiver that the chill factor had dipped to sixty below. The public was advised to travel with a full tank of gas and stay with their cars in the event of breakdown. Jennifer glanced at her gas gauge. She had a quarter of a tank. Plenty. But the aged inadequate heater wheezed out air that was no better than lukewarm, and a stiff chilliness began to settle in her feet as they worked the brake and clutch. She could feel the thick wind tugging at the Beetle's light chassis.

Her nerves were fine and tight, overstretched cords, by the time Philip's gateway loomed at the deserted roadside. The high wrought-iron gate was closed. If it was locked, she wasn't sure what she was going to do.

Wind-drifted snow obscured the twenty or so feet leading to the gate. That meant trouble for the Beetle, so she crushed the accelerator seeking momentum as she made the turn. But it must have been too much momentum, because the little car landed on the driveway with a hop, its rear wheels catching in a hidden ice patch. The car sloughed around, showering snow powder, and spun off the drive, the engine-heavy rear end pulling it down a steep incline into a snowbank.

For Jennifer, there was no time for fear, only a dense vision of a swirling world, a dizzying swing, a tumble backward that ended with a bump. In dumb surprise, she found herself sitting back inclined like an astronaut in an early space capsule. Panic, not plan, made her gun the wheels, burying the rear bumper in another foot of snow.

She was not thinking clearly beyond a shaken inner monologue on her own stupidity when she got out of the car to assess her situation, leaving the engine running. More rattled than she knew, working on automatic reflexes, she stood in the snowbank, locked the door and slammed it shut. Then automatic faded to comprehension and she stared in disbelief at the silver key ring dangling back and forth, separated from her by a pane of glass. The swaying circle mesmerized her, and when it stopped she crossed her arms on the sloping yellow roof, buried her head against the chill fabric of her coat, and moaned in frustration.

The wind snatched the sound; it tore with hooked claws at her rigid back. Her body awoke all at once to the cold. It framed her face in iron, wept like damp acid through her pants, blared in her muscles. Her stadium coat was fine for twenty and thirty degree weather, or for running from car to work to car to house. Tonight, it might have been Kleenex.

Stay with the car. All right. She would run to the mansion, and if Philip wasn't home, she would run back to the car, smash in the window with a rock, and wait inside until help, in some form, arrived.

The large gates were locked, but there was a smaller entrance not far down the wall that was open. She ran down the rutted driveway away from the slanting headlights of her VW, headlights that were shooting aimlessly into the swaying leaf-stripped trees above her head.

I'm a penguin. I'm a penguin. I like cold weather, she thought, trying to dream it, believe in it.

Night closed around her as the drive curved. The stars twinkled in a cloudless black sky, too distant for comfort. The trees arching over the drive seemed in their thrashing malevolence to want to deny her the small solace of the sight of the stars. The wind keened, a predatory chorus.

She had expected the mansion to be close because the lake was out here somewhere, but the drive went on and on. Her breath came in dry puffs. Each step vibrated through her chilled joints in a shock wave.

She pulled her hat over her ears as far as she could, and covered her mouth and nose with the muffler. Her breath made the cashmere damp, then ice-clogged, then raw agony on her flesh. The world was filled with harsh sound: the wind, her breathing, the fluttery scratch of her clothing. Her muscles had begun to contract rhythmically in shivers. As her eye fluids chilled, she tried to walk with her eyes closed but she stumbled in the darkness, falling twice. Even with her eyes open, she could barely make out the lane. The moon was dimmer than it had been a week ago when she was in the forest with Philip, but then, there were many sources of light in a night sky. Philip said so. She ought to be able to see.

I'm a penguin. I don't mind cold weather.

She looked up suddenly and saw it. Lily Hill.

Still distant, it rose from the hilltop, a hard forbidding silhouette. Faint light glowed from etched-glass windows on either side of a grand formal entrance. In the flat moonlight it appeared huge, institutional, charmless. There must be someone home there. There must be. Relations, servants, Doberman pinschers. . . . People didn't leave their mansions unprotected, did they? Her mind fastened on *Upstairs Downstairs*, cataloguing episodes, examining habits of the rich.

The rich didn't strip. Why did he do it? Rebellion? Hard times? How hard could times be if you owned a mansion?

All at once, the snow heaved under her feet. She toppled through an underlying brittle ice crust into two feet of water. The pristine surface had hidden a spring-fed brook.

Like frigid poison, the icy water bled through her clothes, lacerating her raw flesh, washing her in agony, convulsing her muscles. She tried to struggle up, but her burning wrists buckled and she slapped back into the water, her face filling with ice.

When she stood at last, she could hear herself weeping. Pain came in racking paroxysms beyond any threshold she could have imagined. Winded, her body heaving with shudders, she tried to aim her clumsy steps toward the mansion and for the first time, she dazedly realized that she might die. Death. She rarely thought about it. It seemed like something removed from her mundane life, an exotic adventure. But if she didn't get help, she really might die. Her picture would be in the newspapers and people with busy lives would scan the article beneath and say "how sad, she was so young." But dumb. So dumb to have locked her keys in her car on a night when the chill factor was sixty below zero.

There was no exact moment when she realized

that her intellect had begun to malfunction. But distantly, she knew. Her actions pierced her awareness in sharp disconnected detail. Sorcery seemed to transport her from place to place.

She was pounding her fists on the mansion door.

She was trying to break in a window.

She was walking down a country road looking for a mechanic to haul her car out of the ditch.

I'm freezing to death, she thought. Me. Jennifer Hamilton. Won't everyone be surprised . . . She tried to cudgel her mind into coherency. She tried to recall whether she had actually knocked on his door. She tried to think. But thoughts vanished as though someone was plucking them like feathers from her mind.

Where was she? A pretty night waved around her like a diorama in counted cross-stitch: black sky, airy starlight, trees moving in time to a wind that rang like clear crystal.

He almost decided not to come home.

Michele called him to the phone just after he came offstage from the second show. The caller was from his security service with the news that they were picking up an intrusion alarm from his house and asking if he wanted them to notify the police. He told them no, because most of the time it was something innocent. He didn't want the police to have to be chasing around on his property every time the wind tossed a branch on his roof or a wild owl heard Chaucer and went into a territorial frenzy against the kitchen window pane.

He was tired, and sweaty, and tense, and in no

mood to rush outside in arctic temperatures to hunt down a false alarm. But what if it was a group of kids, breaking into the abandoned west wing to party? A commotion would rub Chaucer the wrong way and when roused, the little owl was quite capable of descending, razor-sharp talons poised, on a threatening stranger. Could you live with it, Brooks, if a kid on a lark lost one of his eyes because you didn't want to go out in the cold to check out an alarm?

He arranged for a stand-in and put himself in the car.

The first thing he saw was the ditched Volkswagen, keys in the dead ignition, doors locked, the headlights faded to the pencil-beams of twin flashlights. It could have belonged to anyone. But somehow he knew it was Jennifer's.

The wind's savagery had nearly destroyed the slight dents of her footprints leading up his drive. Fear nourished his impulse to break out in a run, following them. But he made himself get back into the station wagon; he made himself go slowly up the drive to be sure the dim trail didn't lead off into the trees. He had spent years learning to decipher tracks, and as though she had left a story for him in copperplate, he could see each stumble, each time she had rested or paused in confusion. The pressure of an accelerating pulse stabbed his throat; his heartbeat became militant, electric. The phrase, his phrase "come see me—you know where to look" came back at him like a whip. Where had he expected her to come? The Cougar Club?

Her waifish figure finally appeared in his headlights, limping in a ragged ellipse about twenty yards from his front door. He floored the accelerator and spun up the drive, slamming the transmission into park, running up to her.

Frost covered her in sparkling dust. It rimmed her eyes with blue-white lashes. It was imbedded into her clothing like mica in a sidewalk. When he lifted her face, her pansy petal eyes stared up at him unknowingly.

"I'm looking at . . ." She squinted at the shining ice crystals on her sleeve. "Snowflakes." Her voice was hoarse, small and slurred.

Shock? Delirium? He tried to remember everything he knew about hypothermia. His mind threw up a blank screen. His shooting heartbeat set the rhythm for his instinctive response. He swept her up in his arms and began racing with her toward the house. In his adrenalized state, she was no heavier than a toy.

Her arms came sloppily around his neck, falling like broken pieces of stick candy. "I'm a penguin." Her head flopped hard onto his shoulder. "I like cold weather."

Jenny. Jenny. Hang on, darling. Hypothermia. What do I know about hypothermia? In warmblooded animals, enzymatic reactions take place properly only within a set range of temperatures. When prolonged chilling forced the body's temperature down too long, the chemical processes began to misfire. Muscles grew lax—the heart was a muscle. . . .

Supporting her limp weight in one hand, he dragged open the front door and lifted her inside. She murmured incoherently as he carried her upstairs through the blocks of indigo moonlight on the landing. He booted open his bedroom door and set her down on his bed where she lay on his yellow quilt like a broken doll. His hand slipped under the muffler to touch her cheek. It might have been ice.

He grabbed the receiver of his bedside phone and dialed rapidly, forcing the dial. When it began to ring he tucked it into his shoulder and started to pry at the ice-encrusted zipper of her coat. Her clothes, moisture saturated, had frozen to rigidity. An anonymous voice came on the phone and informed him, after he asked, that Dr. Campell wasn't available. He's with a woman, Philip thought. He snapped out that this was Philip Brooks and an emergency. The bland voice advised him glumly that he would be connected.

In the extended delay, he unwrapped the frosty muffler from her face and realized that it was his. Staring at it, he had the utterly stupid feeling that he might begin to cry.

Jack's voice. "I don't know who the hell this is but it better be important."

"Jack, this is Philip. Can you come over?"

"Philip?" The voice sharpened. "What's going on? Are you all right?"

"Yes. Jenny's with me. I found her outside. She looks like a snow cone."

Even more sharply, "Is she conscious?"

"Semiconscious."

"Other symptoms?" Jack snapped out.

"Ataxia, dysarthria, disorientation. And her damn zipper is frozen shut."

"Steady. All right? What's her pulse?"

He dragged off her mitten and found her wrist. "Dear God, I can't find one."

"Be calm, Philip." The voice became deliberately

healing, stern, sustaining. "If she's semiconscious she's alive and she's got a pulse. Maybe it's thready, but you'll find it. I'll be there in a minute. Pull her clothes off and put her under a blanket. *Don't* put her in a hot tub. *Don't* put her in a heating blanket, or you may throw her into shock. Did you catch all that?"

"Yes. What about an ambulance?"

"We'll decide when I get there." The line went dead.

The thawing zipper broke free and as he brought it down past her waist, he saw her wide-set eyes focus on him with sudden lucidity.

"What's ataxia?" The words were quite clear, but very hoarse.

"Jenny? Sweetheart, this is Philip. Do you know me?"

"Ataxia," prompted the blue lips softly.

"It means loss of coordination," he told her gently.

"Thanks." The barely audible word was sardonic. She seemed to be trying to smile. "Dysarthria?"

"Slurred speech."

"Why do you know those words?"

He raised her shoulders enough to drag her coat off. "I'm a biologist."

"Biologist. Biologist." She gave the word various amazed inflections.

He had a moment to be elated over that evidence of rationality before her eyes closed and she seemed to drift again. She shivered so pitifully it wrenched his heart. He would have given everything to be able to take her pain.

All the way to his fingertips he could feel the

pressure of his emotions as he began to open her blouse. Her dazed husky whisper startled him.

"Philip . . . Are you going to make love to me?"

"Yes, God help us both." He touched a shaken kiss to her cold brow. "When you're better."

Her heavy lashes dropped, her fist curled drowsily near her cheek as he undressed and dried her. She seemed to have fallen into a light sleep under his wool blanket when he carried her damp clothes to the bathroom. He returned to find her wandering around his bedroom with the blanket wrapped around her, trailing it behind her like a besotted monk.

"I have to find a mechanic," she rasped softly, gazing vaguely around the room. "I have to get my . . ." She thought about it for a long time—"my 'wagon fixed."

He smiled for the first time since he had walked away from her in the library, and scooped her up, a droll, weightless bundle, depositing her back on the bed, nuzzling his face in her damp hair. "I'll fix your wagon but good if you don't stay still."

For Jennifer, consciousness returned at broken intervals as though the world were a thing seen through erratically swinging shutters.

Distantly she saw herself clinging to Philip's arm and heard her own excited rambling. "Philip, I was lost in the freezing cold. I had an adventure. . . . I faced *death*." Someone was trying to put something in her mouth. "I knew it wasn't dark, because you told me about all the light in the night sky—besides the moon and the stars there's air glow . . . all the light from outside the galaxy—faint stars, interstellar dust. . . ."

Her jaw was taken in a firm grip and she found herself staring into a vaguely familiar face, with amused gray eyes and tousled curls. She was told sternly, "Oral temperatures are unreliable enough in your condition. Either keep this under your tongue, young lady, or it's going in your rear end. No matter what Philip says."

Pained tears spilled, she found the comfort of Philip's chest, the thermometer went under her tongue. She drifted.

She woke once with warm hands feeling her pulse, stroking her hair. The hand that led her to consciousness was gentle, as was the voice calling her name, but it hurt to be awake. The light in the room was dim. But even that stung her eyes.

A soft voice said, "She's adorable. Lucky you. Have you made her a happy woman yet?"

"I've made her a confused woman. I've made her a frightened woman. As you see, I've made her a very ill woman. But no, I haven't made her a happy woman."

"All these years I've known you, and here I've always thought nothing got to you except injured wildlife. You were so well vaccinated against women by the time you were fifteen. Personally, I'm in favor of anyone who can make you feel like a human being again. What do you think it's doing to the people who love you, watching you cut yourself off like this?" The attractive male voice developed a sudden impatience that seemed rooted in pain. "All right, I understand why you wouldn't take the vice-presidency in your uncle's company. But when you know I'd give you all kinds of money . . . Don't give me that look of yours. I'm not going to resurrect that hopeless battle."

A silence grew and stretched.

Two minutes or two hours later she opened her eyes. Her field of vision was blurred, distorted. An ornate plasterwork ceiling swung above her head. The walls were lovely, elaborate with gilt touches. There was a massive carved marble hearth with a stuffed owl on it. She had the strangest feeling that she had been transported back in history like the heroine in a time travel romance. This room came straight out of the Victorian era.

The detail of the owl bothered her. It seemed incongruous. She closed her eyes again, experiencing a wash of nauseating discomfort. Her skin felt as though it had been seared. Every muscle, every joint in her body cried out for mercy. And her head throbbed, throbbed, throbbed.

"I'll listen to her heart again if you promise not to accuse me of trying to feel her up," came a man's voice.

Philip's soft laugh answered the voice. "Never. I know they wean you off all those inconvenient desires in medical school."

"That's a myth and a half." A chair sighed under shifting weight. "If you could see the luscious body I just left unsatisfied . . ."

"Really? Then you did finish things before I called?"

The first man responded with quiet appreciative laughter and threw something—a pillow.

Jennifer felt the bedclothes shift over her and the robe—she realized she was wearing a robe now—gently rearranged. The hard circle of the stethoscope pressed beneath her breast. She opened her eyes again, gazing beyond dark curls at the stuffed owl on the mantel. This time, though, it seemed to have its head turned to the side. She closed her eyes with an inward moan.

"Beautiful heartbeat," said the voice from the dark curls. "I kiss my fingers to it. Come and listen. You'll feel much better." The stethoscope rattled as it came away from his ears. "What did I tell you? She's young and healthy. She probably won't even catch a cold on you."

The bed shifted; a graceful hip curved against hers. After a moment, the metal disc was removed and her robe was carefully closed, the blankets pulled up around her neck. She blinked her eyes open and focused on Philip Brooks. Pale light haloed the corn silk hair. The sparkling blue eyes held her in a thorough study.

"Jenny?"

"I just happened to be in the neighborhood," she rasped weakly. "So I thought I'd drop by and freeze to death on your front lawn."

She just had time to see the smile enter his eyes before she had to close her own in exhausted effort. She felt him bring his index finger slowly down her cheek, his touch skimming like a breath.

"They've redone Oz in Victorian," she breathed.

"Believe it or not, love, this is my bedroom. And this is the one way I never imagined getting you into it."

All she had left was a tiny whisper. "At least I was carried over the threshold." She opened her eyes one last time because she couldn't resist seeing whether she made him smile again. But her gaze, weak and random, fell instead on the mantel—and registered the fact that the stuffed owl was gone. Had she been seeing things?

"Philip . . ." she began, trying to tell him about it, though she could feel a trickle of weary tears on her cheeks.

His lips removed the light moisture. "Don't worry about anything, Jenny." His hand touched her hair. "I'm taking care of you. Sleep."

Behind her closed eyelids, she could sense the room falling suddenly into darkness, but his hand still stroked her hair.

Seven

She woke again to an unearthly glow. White
sunlight blazed through the shutters in long narrow beams, bouncing like smoky spears from every surface. Warmth permeated the air with the
sweet lavendery scent of age. As she inhaled and
stretched the beguiling mixture seemed to reach
deeply inside her, healing parts of her that had
always felt unfledged and cold and lonely. She was
in Philip's bedroom.

Last night's memories returned in liquid pictures, as though she were seeing their undulating
reflection in a puddle. She had been cold, then
horribly cold—and then cared for.

Philip's bedroom. Looking around her, she tried
to absorb some sense of him from the things
around her. She had never seen a room like this,
except roped off with velvet cord in a museum.
The colors, melting together with archaic elegance,
could have been drawn from an Alma-Tadema

canvas. From a yellow ceiling sank a frieze and cornice of violet and gold. Harmonizing violet and yellow silk covered the walls. The somber gold draperies matched the upholstery of a lounge and an easy chair with a footstool. Taste had evolved in ninety years and it surprised her that no one had ever redecorated this pretty room. To the un-accustomed modern eye, it seemed strange and yet pleasing, romantic. She lifted her hand to touch the exquisitely carved butternut headboard above her, enjoying the milky smooth texture of the polished wood.

Pain returned as she sat up, brief burning spasms in her muscles that died into stiffness. She noticed her clothes, intimately draped on the lounge seat in a ray of sunlight.

Her pink blouse on top of the pile heaved sud-denly as the earth might under a burgeoning vol-cano and a small face with furious yellow eyes erupted from between her blouse buttons.

She screamed. It came out as a throttled unsat-isfying squeak so she screamed again.

That one did the trick. She heard a door open and running footsteps filled the corridor. Philip shot into the room, his long-boned feet bare, his soft cotton jeans teasing the outline of his marvel-ous legs. His hair was tousled from the passage of the blue-flecked wool sweater he was dragging on.

"Jennifer? What happened?"

His blue eyes were focusing on her with thrill-ing anxiety, and she wanted just to stare and stare into them. A band of lean, rock-hard stom-ach still showed above his pants, and his hands pulled absently at the sweater, covering the golden flesh. She swallowed and pointed.

"An owl!"

It seemed reasonable to expect a decent show of alarm. But showing no alarm at all, Philip strode across the room to the owl, whose head had swiveled sideways to look at him.

"Did you scare her, you bad old bird?" he reproached. "I told you I didn't want you in here."

The bad old bird gave him back a stern look and hopped to the chair arm, then took off to the top of a lofty butternut highboy with a bit of pink cloth in one claw. Standing on one leg, it held out the claw to solemnly inspect the bit of material.

"My underpants," she gasped.

"C'mon, Chaucer. Fork 'em over," Philip said, standing below the indifferent owl, looking up in exasperation. He turned back to her with a wry look that apologized. "I think he's infatuated."

"With my underpants, maybe. You mean you *know* this bird? Why do you call him Chaucer?"

"He loves Chaucer." He pulled a green-bound volume from a bookcase over his desk and opened it to show her a fan of shredded pages. "Not only is he fond of medieval literature, he's also acquiring a taste for modern fiction." He showed her a ragged copy of *For Whom the Bell Tolls.* She began to grin as a lone page drifted desolately to the floor. "An eclectic appetite. His best job was on the first copy of my late great dissertation. He sees himself as quite the editor."

She was registering the fact of his dissertation as Chaucer bobbed and poked his head through the leg opening of her underpants, straightening to strut deadpan across the top of the highboy, the underpants draped around his tiny feathery body like a loosely wrapped toga.

She dropped her head between her bent knees, giving a spurt of laughter, her hand falling protectively over her head. She heard Philip speak to the owl.

"I haven't seen such a display of uncouth manners since the lecture I gave at the women's club when you regurgitated a pellet into the chairperson's teacup." There was a second's delay, and then a muffled howl of laughter breached the bedclothes. He turned to see her shaking, her shoulders heaving, her fists banging in soft thumps on the back of her head.

"I thought . . ." Her words dissolved into more laughter. She fought for breath. "I thought . . . Philip, Mrs. Buckner, the women's club president, was in the library yesterday and I heard her telling Annette that you had given this *wonderful* program at the club. She was praising your expertise to the skies and saying what an education it had been for her. She said she'd learned more about animal nature in that half hour than she had in the previous ten years." More groaning laughter. "I was so stupid. I thought she was talking about your stage act, and I thought humph! what kind of a town is this anyway?"

He watched her emerge from the vise of her knees, her face deep pink, her eyes shining with hidden tears that were not from the laughter. He wanted to go to her and kiss her. The terry robe was hanging open and he wanted to draw it slowly down over her arms—but it was too soon. Yesterday he had learned where his impatience could push her.

She rubbed her face with her palms, trying to calm the hot jumpiness inside. Her eyes were wet and irritated. She could feel her own idiotically wide smile pushing at her cheeks, but there was nothing she could do about it. It felt fused to her face; indelible. "You have an owl for a pet."

"I have an owl for a pest. I don't believe in people keeping wild animals in their homes so you see I'm a big hypocrite. Laws protect wildlife from that. But I have a license to keep Chaucer. He's disabled. One of his claws doesn't have much of a grip to it, and he'd have a hard time picking up as much prey as he'd need in the wild."

Gazing at the top of the highboy, she was falling in love with the pixieish creature who was tearing her underpants into a thousand pieces. Her gaze flew back to Philip, hitching his desk chair to the bed beside her, sitting backward on it with his arms crossed on the top, his chin at rest on his forearms. Vivid blue eyes gazed back inquiringly into hers.

A stinging lightness rose in her stomach. Her chest held an excited flutter. She was aware suddenly that her body underneath the robe was naked, a sensation that was not unpleasant, but embarrassing. His steady regard was polite, unhurried, yet she found herself stalling as though he had just put her under some vague pressure.

"You said you were a biologist," she said.

"A wildlife biologist. I'm surprised you remember that."

His eyes had begun to make her cheeks hot. She started to say "thank you for last night" but there was something a bit awkward and suggestive about that phrase, so she tried, "I'm going to cherish every moment. I've always wanted to be rescued. Thanks for thawing me out."

A half smile. A long searching glance. "*That* we've just begun to work on." He noticed her hand lying at her side, the restless fingers pinching up the bedclothes into an array of little pyramids.

"My luck. I go to give myself to a man and end up with my car imbedded in a snowbank, and half frozen to death." The words came blurting out.

His reply was immediate. "Is that why you came? To give yourself to me?"

"I thought those were your terms."

Her gaze, trying to stay with his, kept sliding somewhere to the vicinity of his elbow. The blankets at her side looked like a landscape of the Nile Valley. There was a sudden desperate need inside him to make this easier for her, easier than her fierce sensitivity would allow, easier than the inconvenient sense of urgency in his own body seemed to dictate.

"I take back my terms."

"Too late. I'm here." She had wanted the words to sound calm. They came out a little too quickly, too loudly. She felt exhausted and elated at one time. There. It was out. The lot cast, the die tossed. You've heard of the girl who can't say no? she thought. Well, she just said yes. Help! Staring distractedly at the relaxed suppleness of his wrist where it emerged from the blue sweater, she tried to brazen it out. "You've already had the opportunity to undress me once."

Fresh oxygen stretched the waiting flame he had been attempting to contain. "It seemed like a good idea to get some practice in ahead of time."

She observed that he had beautiful wrist bones. "So. How did I look?"

"Pardon me?"

She made a soft ahem. "I asked you: how did I look?"

Jennifer Hamilton, the world may never see your like again. How had she looked? He tried to dredge up some kind of a picture but all that came to him was a recollection of wounded brown eyes that seemed not to know him and chilled, blue-white flesh. Looking at her body when it became pink and healthy from his lovemaking, that would mean something; *how* it looked meant nothing at all. It was her. Her body. The only one he wanted. Details of size and shape were immaterial. However, that would hardly make a poetic declaration. He could feel the anxiety behind her defensive bravado reaching out to him, twisting his heart. She needed to know that he found her physically attractive, and God knew he did, whether it was significant to him or not. So, even though he had no clear recollection of the tantalizing form under his blankets, he said, "You're lovely. Very, very lovely. Centerfold material."

"You don't think my thighs are a little . . ." Her fingers produced and destroyed several more pyramids. "You know, fat?" Her gaze stuck in a fascinated way on the corner of his mouth that was working hard not to turn upward. "Well, I mean, when it's summer, and I'm wearing shorts, when I'm sitting on park benches my thighs sort of spread out and I think, gee, maybe I should sit on the edge of the bench so they won't"—she gulped—"do that." She watched the edges of his mouth give up the struggle. His eyes had become warm, the irises clear and brilliant. This is very cathartic, she thought. He might as well know right away what an idiot I am.

"Maybe I should take another look," he suggested playfully. His hand came to the edge of the blanket and curled around it, his fingers electric on the upper swell of her breast.

Instinctively she held the blanket in place, though it was not what she wanted. Nerves. His hand left the blanket; a finger touched with sweet brevity on her lips. Then the hand rested on her thigh, massaged her in a slow circle, smoothed gently over the slight roundness between her legs, caressed the other thigh. Her throat had become tight and arid and she realized that her thighs were clenched together. She almost wept when the hand left her.

"Great thighs," he said.

"Do you think my nipples are a funny color?" she asked quickly, hoping he'd explore them too.

At first he'd thought she was a mere one in a thousand. Now he saw she was probably one in a million. Her nipples he hadn't forgotten. Kissing her like a kid in the front seat of his car, he had learned their erect contour against his flesh and his palm registered the memory with a slight shock in the spot that had touched her. His hand curved unconsciously, recalling how perfectly her breast had nestled there. He realized what he was doing and shoved the hand in his pocket. Oh, Lord, he thought, I hope I don't attack her.

"Your nipples match your lips." He brought his hand from his pocket to brush his fingers over her mouth, barely touching. "The shade of roses at twilight. So. As I've officially approved your thighs and nipples and you've presumably seen enough of me to know what you're getting, will you stay with me?"

His hand cooled her cheek, his thumb lazily stroking the rise of her cheekbone. Her respiratory machinery seemed to be operating on a broken current.

"If I . . . that is, if we . . . together—" She took a steadying breath. "I mean, if we were together, it wouldn't be your first time, would it? I mean, obviously. Right?"

Touched and rather taken aback by the question, he answered gently, "No. It wouldn't."

"Is this different? Different from the other times?"

"Altogether different." He wasn't sure if she believed him. Words would never be enough. The kaleidoscope of emotions in her face was too complicated to be dissected simply. How could there be such longing in eyes that had a tendency to stare at him like he was about to hurt her? He wanted to cleanse those eyes of fear. He was almost overcome by the urge to slide his terry robe off her shoulders and make her naked. But that wasn't going to convince her that this was different. Instead he made himself stand and smile briskly at her. "Well. Breakfast. Your clothes are still on the damp side. Want to borrow something of mine?"

She looked a little less terrified walking down the staircase beside him belted into a clean pair of his jeans, her unbound breasts swaying against the cotton fabric under his long-sleeved T-shirt. Two pairs of wool socks held on his running shoes. Knowing that she couldn't possibly have on any underpants was hard on his libido so he labored to perish the thought. She was moving stiffly, sore from the stresses of hypothermia on her muscles, but her expression was bright and engaging as she gazed in wordless awe around her.

"Nice little place you've got here," she said, as though it made her uncomfortable.

"It's a bear to heat. Maybe you should have a sweater too. Are you cold?"

She wasn't, not really, but something in his eyes made a shiver scamper up her spine and she hugged herself. His arm came around her, tucking her against his body as they walked.

"You could have a fresh egg for breakfast. I'll take you to see my chicken."

Shyly, she put her hand up to take hold of his fingers. "You have chickens instead of etchings?"

"One chicken."

After a sweep of breathtaking, empty rooms, they were in a large sunny pantry lined with fresh newspapers. Philip got down on one knee in a pool of flaxen sunlight. In front of him was a short square house with protruding straw and he looked as if he were about to propose to it.

"Henrietta . . ." His voice was musical, coaxing. His tongue clicked beguilingly.

A beak emerged from the doorway, and the bright bead of an eye, and then a small brown hen plunged out at a fast strut and ran comically across the floor to Philip. He slapped his thigh several times and she hopped up there, clucking contentedly as he stroked her feathers and cooed blandishments at her.

" 'Morning, Henrietta. What have you been up to, hmmm?" The hen put back her head and luxuriated in having her neck scratched. "Did you lay an egg for Jenny? Good girl . . . Clever girl . . ." His hand slid over the polished feathers on her back. "The wildlife rehabilitation people in Milwaukee found her in a crowded city park when she was a tiny ball of fluff, and thought maybe she was a bobwhite. They brought her to me hoping I'd be able to rear her so she could be returned to the wild. Of course, with my great store of book-learning, I told them no way is this a bobwhite; this is a quail. I don't know quite how she grew up to be a chicken. Do you, sweetie? Why'd you grow into a chicken?"

Since the last two sentences had regressed to a coo, Jennifer assumed the questions were directed at the hen rather than at her. As she watched his enchanting, if slightly besotted, attentions to the small bird, an unsettled feeling grew within her. She loved him. She loved this man. She was afraid at first to experience the emotion, and held the knowledge at an intellectual level, resisting it, fighting to keep it from impacting her senses. Then the walls weakened and collapsed, and it flooded into her, each sensation sure and strong. What had made him like this, as gracious, as appealing inside as he was outside? The sensations kept flowing powerfully as though they were fed by some deep spring. She became desperate in her need to feel the tactile richness of his lips against her, to touch his hair and let it stream through her fingers like gold webbing.

"During summer I have her out-of-doors quite a bit, but we have a couple of foxes around so I've never built her a pen out there." His sentence rolled to a halt and it occurred to him abruptly that he had been going on and on about Henrietta and he glanced up at Jennifer's face. "Why are you smiling at me like that?"

"Because. Because you're such a . . . such a . . ." Love sent an avalanche of nibbling attacks throughout her body. Catching Philip off guard, she tumbled him on his back as her mouth pressed against his and the brown hen took off squawking. Hotly, with glutted sweetness, they clung together, his laughter bringing soft gusts of breath against her mouth. Warmth radiated upward from his ribcage, infusing her breasts with a pleasant heaviness. The rhythm of his laughter caressed her nipples.

"What am I, Jenny?" His mouth began to initiate a new, deeper contact. "Tell me what I am."

His hands held the sides of her body just under her arms, his palms water-soft and stirring against the edges of her breasts. Her sensitivity there, her desire to be enclosed in the valley of his fingers overwhelmed her and she depressed herself against his chest. His hands tightened, pressing inward, and the temperature of her body seemed to fluctuate.

"A surprise." Her words were whispers that rose between his heart-stopping kisses. "Why . . ." Her breath ran out as his knee bent, coming easily upward to ride the warm space between her thighs. She gasped out, "Why—do you like birds?"

He showered little kisses across her upper lip. "They fly."

"Chickens don't fly." Her voice was high and light, a trickle of sound. Her body moved against his, searching, trying to sate itself, acknowledging the hard angles, the silken planes.

"Don't . . . get . . . technical," he breathed, pushing her away gently enough to bring his hands to the softness of her that was searing into his chest.

Instead of a handful of her, he received a handful of chicken feathers. Henrietta wriggled between their separate chests, cackling affectionately, tickling their faces with a cloud of feathers. Jennifer descended into a laughing, hiccuping bundle at his side, and his hand stroking her face discovered that her lashes were damp. Nerve chills played up her back. In spite of the laughter, her body reflected distress. The cheerful smile, the bright manner were deceptive. She had endured a lot last night, and it was still with her. Too much, too quickly. He chided himself for not having fed her breakfast yet.

She had barely finished laughing when Philip got to his feet and, smiling, helped her to stand. He said nothing, just caressed her under the chin. She was beginning to feel like one of his birds. She had learned more about sexual frustration since meeting Philip Brooks than from everything else that she had experienced in her life previously. Why had he stopped? All right, the chicken. But they could have gone back upstairs.

She watched him make her breakfast in a peaceful room lined halfway to the ceiling with hand-painted Delft tile. Chaucer rode on his head, preening his hair into something that looked like it had been through a cyclone.

Sitting with her knees drawn up on a bentwood chair, eyeing him curiously, she asked, "Did you know that you're extraordinarily good-looking?" Maybe it was a stupid question.

It seemed to startle him. He paused in the act of chopping bacon into an omelet, and tossed a glance at her. "No. But hum a few bars and I'll fake it. Is this a test?"

She couldn't help being fascinated that he was touchy about it. "No. What do you see in the mirror?"

He turned back to the bacon. "Adult male homo sapiens, reasonable skeletal alignment, two eyes, one on either side of a nose, average dentition, medium height."

"Oh boy. I hope *I* don't ever look in that mirror if that's what it does to *you*."

That drew an unwilling smile. "I have a friend—Darrell—who says it was wasted on me. He says I could have been a short pot-bellied guy with hornrimmed glasses and never known the difference. He's probably right."

"You don't think there are such things as beautiful and plain?"

"Not to the degree most people seem to. I find it difficult to get excited about the cosmetic value of differences that amount to a few millimeters in facial structure."

"Well, I guess I know now how *not* to excite you," she said, and saw that symphony of a smile fasten on her.

"Your millimeters are an exception." He was fending Chaucer off the bacon with one hand.

"I suppose you think it's relative? Aardvarks think aardvarks are pretty?"

"That would sum it up nicely."

Which seemed to be all he had to say on the subject of having a face that made the world stop and stare. The love inside her never stopped flowing. Once she had decided to accept it, the rest came naturally. She moved through the day like a hovercraft, never touching earth. Love, she discovered, had a strange effect on the body. Shivers pulsed through her at his slightest touch. She had body aches from the yearning.

Well-fed, they went to his attic, where rising warmth made the air soft and luminous. A shining lacework of frost sparkled on semicircular windows. Light in bright colors from a stained glass skylight broadcast itself onto quiet surfaces.

Everything here was magical: Japanese lacquered cabinets, oil lamps, clocks and urns, a Victorian pram, beautiful boxes filled with postcard collections, antique toys, Art Nouveau jewelry from Tiffany and Cartier.

On a chintz settee in a window alcove, he showed her a stereoptic viewer—a tin binocular-like instrument that made the pictures on its special viewing cards come to life in three dimensions. There were scenes of buildings devastated by the 1906 San Francisco earthquake, sentimental pictures of puppies at play with little girls in lace and ringlets, a young couple in neck-to-toe nightdresses grinning lasciviously at each other as they stood before a canopied bed. The title: "Married At Last."

The photograph albums that he reluctantly let her see revealed a great deal about the Brookses in all their luster. Philip as a child standing at a tilt in front of the Leaning Tower of Pisa. Philip skiing in Austria; Philip on yachts, in private stables with his pony, playing football on the White House lawn. Philip with loving parents and grandparents. There were no pictures of him beyond the age of sixteen.

The obvious question would have been about the money. Being Jennifer, she didn't ask it.

"I have a deep dark secret," she said, and set the photograph album on the settee between them.

He took in the slight unsteadiness of her hands, the downcast glance, the set lips. She's going to tell me she's a virgin, he thought, and tried to prepare some remark that was light, comforting.

"I'm illegitimate."

Her words were simply spoken, emotionless, but they lacerated his next four heartbeats. In the forest, that was what she had been trying to tell him. That explanation for her reticence, her tiptoeing backward caution about life had never occurred to him. Perhaps it was because of the very unassuming ordinariness she seemed to project of a tame life passed without trauma. Silently, he praised the parent who had given her that, under less than normal circumstances.

"That's something else I don't believe in," he said. "Illegitimacy. Children are always legitimate." Her face didn't change. Trite comfort, he thought. Language was an imprecise, unsophisticated tool, useless against the sparks of sadness that must exist among her memories. It appalled him that she had to sit there in her immaculate integrity and make that confession as though it stained her. Dick, Jane, and Spot, Mother and Father . . . If that image was changing, it was too late for Jennifer. Already she was beginning to look embarrassed, as though she was sorry she had told him, and had put him under the obligation of saying something kind. Plainly, pity frightened her.

"Did you know your father?"

"No. He's dead now. We saw his obituary in a Chicago paper. He was a traveling salesman." She grinned a little. "It's kind of funny, really. Mom was, well, not a farmer's daughter, but her dad ran a feed store. To this day, he hasn't quite warmed up to my appearance in the world." Her hands, forgotten on her knees, began to slide up and down over her kneecaps, massaging the denim as though she needed to restore circulation in the flesh below. "True tinges of black humor, wouldn't you say? My mother never accepted sympathy. She turned it around by thrusting her palm to her forehead and staggering melodramatically to the couch, saying in thrilling tones, 'I was se-duced and abandoned!' And then she'd ask me if I'd finished my homework. But I could sense the pain inside." She paused. Her hands became still. "It ended happily because last November she went to Madison to become a speechwriter for the gover-nor and she has a wonderful boyfriend who's a lawyer. . . . but there are days when I'll wake up and look outside at a gray sky and think that maybe my birth came from a dirty joke."

He had wanted to let her talk on and on to him about it, to let it spill out and away from her and be rid of it. Her last words seemed to pierce some unknown pain threshold in his soul and he reached out, lifting her close to his body, holding her with crushing tightness. Her head curled against his chest, her hands caught and held on to his sweater. Presently, the dark emotions began to recede and he picked up her hands and began abstractedly to warm them with his breath. Dear God, she's never going to be able to stand it that I strip. What in the name of heaven am I going to do?

Her voice, obstinate in its lack of expression, cut into his thoughts.

"I don't usually tell people."

"Why should you?"

Her head tipped against his shoulder, looking up at him. "I thought you should know. In case it mattered."

He tried hard to keep a straight face. He tried so hard that his jaw felt like it was turning to cement. At times, she seemed to come right out of Jane Austen. Finally, it was partly his savage anxiety about her, partly the Elizabeth Bennett sincerity in those brown eyes that did him in and he began to laugh, and kept laughing even though his side had begun to ache and she had punched him a couple of times on the shoulder.

"Jenny, darling," he gasped, "I'm sorry, I'm truly sorry. But do you think you've confused me with Fitzwilliam Darcy?" That drew him another round of pummeling. She was laughing now too, her eyes alight with indignation, though her facial muscles had relaxed like a child's. Gathering her head in the curve of his hand, he brought her parted lips inch by inch to his, pressing her again and again into his slow open kiss. Their eyelashes drifted against each other's skin like damp brushes. Her lips shone intoxicatingly with their joining moisture. Desire ran through him like torch fire. Thought expired. *Now, Jenny. Love, I can't wait anymore. I can't wait.* His hand had started to slip to her breast when she spoke to him, her voice quiet, love-slurred.

"Philip?"

"Hmm?" he murmured tenderly.

"Others might care. Some of your relatives."

Oh, God, he thought. She's still thinking about it. For all the kindling responsiveness of her body, part of her mind remained in the shadows. His body was so filled with the red mist of wanting her that most of him seemed to be floating. Half the fluids in his body felt like they'd buried themselves into the part of him that wanted to bury itself in her. If she'd been any other woman, he would have let nature roll on its own sweet, inevitable course to avoid the cost of subduing his fiery body. But this was Jenny. For Jenny, he had to make everything right. Some of his relatives, she had said.

"No one I'm interested in," he murmured, and was relieved to see the bruised eyes warm. He wanted to shower her sensitivity with gifts, to crowd her memories with so much joy that the blackness would draw back like a tide and tremble at its own lack of significance.

He stood, cradling her to his chest, carried her to a Java teak wardrobe and set her lightly down.

"Since we're up here, would you like to climb into something prettier than my jeans?"

Eight

When jeans encased his incredible legs, there really was no prettier garment in the world, she thought. She had been burning since breakfast to climb out of the jeans she'd borrowed from him and into his arms. The problem was, she had done about everything that seemed possible for a basically shy person to initiate that. Loving someone was no longer an abstract dream. He was here with her, his company a giddy delight. Every part of him seemed touchable, inviting. In her lifetime, she had never wanted anything as badly as she wanted him at this moment. She smiled at him as he opened the wardrobe, but she could feel the tautness in her mouth, and the jittery nerve-thrills within.

Inside the cedar-lined teak cabinet was a world of costume that rivaled free access to a storeroom of historic dress at the Smithsonian. There were top hats, satin opera slippers, umbrellas in black

silk, handpainted evening gloves, beaded evening
bags, huge elegant hats with flowers or plumes
and veils. Gowns in rich textiles glowed like old
gems in the delicate attic light.

She laughed when he put a top hat on her
head, and remembered that she had been Abe
Lincoln the first time his mouth, with its softness
and eroticism, had closed over hers.

Then with the abandon of children dressing up,
they turned the lovely clothes into play. She
peacocked in a black velvet evening cloak, her
eyes finding his over a gold ostrich fan. He lounged
indolently in a chair like an Edwardian rake, a
brown derby hat tipped forward over his eyes,
quizzing her figure through opera glasses. She let
the cloak slide to the floor, and with her heart
beating wildly, caught a handful of fabric at her
back and tugged the T-shirt tight, very tight over
her breasts, making her nipples stand out in delectable arrogant points. The bowler hat toppled,
the opera glasses fell lightly to the Persian carpet
at his feet, and Philip slithered from the chair as
though his spine had turned to jelly. The tumble
was a masterpiece of athletic grace. She joined
him quickly on the floor, reviving him with a
mink muff rubbed teasingly against his cheek.

A lazily heated smile glittered in the blue eyes.
He took the muff from her, sliding his hand inside it, and put it to her cheek. Then his lips
replaced the muff, wandering over her skin to
lightly caress her mouth. Long sleepy kisses
followed, a feast of sensation, suffusing her body
with liquid heaviness. He did not touch her
intimately, but she felt the growing tautness there,
deep, a flaring pressure. Gently he brought the

muff back to her cheek, massaging her flesh with the dense fur. The massage wandered to her nape, the fur raising little welts of pleasure down the length of her spine. He played the fur over her scalp, and in slow erotic circles on her back, following her hips, the curves of her bottom. His kiss sank into her, a repeated motion, his body angling slightly away to permit his hands access to the front of her. Her body curled toward his hand as the fur stroked her stomach, and then, softly, her breasts. One of his hands tugged at the T-shirt, drawing it up until she was uncovered for him and the mink tingled over her breasts, whetting her nipples to a hypersensitivity that made the air against them have texture. Her mouth was deeply open to him, her skin tender. Her body writhed against his hand as it traveled over her jeans, sliding over her thighs, her belly, between her legs.

Her skin was feverish, her eyes as overbright as his when he swept her to her feet.

"Will you dance with me now, Jenny love?" He laughed, probably at her expression. His breath came in short gasps that sounded as though he were trying to bring them under his control. "Don't look like that. . . ." More thick laughter. "I love you. Let's dance. Just like this. It'll feel so good—wait. Come here, darling. . . ."

He pulled a gown from the wardrobe, a fairy-tale creation from the turn of the century, of biscuit-colored chiffon with drifts of Valenciennes lace. He held it to her, smiling, and she saw in a daze that the shade matched her skin. Her legs barely held her as she dressed in it behind the clouds and winged cherubs of a French giltwood screen.

Quavering, her heart aloft, she ran back to the exhilarating strength of his arms.

Honeyed melodies from the early years of the century drifted from a gramophone with a mahagony horn and the room swirled with color and sound. His voice softly taught her the steps but it was his hands and his body that guided her into them, making the movements simple and direct, a blur of pleasure.

The bouquet of cedar and floral potpourri from her gown enclosed them like the perfume of a spray of flowers. Their bare feet streamed against the warm oak floor, making soft sounds. Her naked skin under the gown felt the slippery fabric move over it in fluid swirls. Her silk petticoats rustled, caressing his legs. They seemed to be free-falling, then blended together, their bodies exquisite against each other in their heightened state of sensual awareness. Each brush together was dulcet, golden.

He stepped back from her, holding her fingers in a light clasp, and the warmth in her body centered, humming, in her fingers where he touched her. She was a little shaky, but the sensation was delightful, and her pulse became a slow uncertain rhythm, holding time as his mouth bent to hers in a nectarous whisper.

He drew her to a velvet chair that stood by a desk inlaid with marquetry.

"This was my great-grandmother's desk." His breath grazed her skin like a petal. "When I was little, she used to sit beside me at this desk and make me practice my signature, because she said I was going to be an important man and I should have an impressive signature for the momentous

documents I was going to be required to sign."
His smile registered the memory. "And—she said
—a gentleman should be able to write beautiful
love letters to all his mistresses." The blue eyes
held apology and amusement. His unsteady fingers rested for a moment on her cheek. "I'm afraid
a few of her notions were on the outdated side. I
do keep the inkwell filled, though." He took a pen
from a compartment in a gold-mounted inkstand
and dipped it twice in the lapis inkwell. "As things
turned out, no major bills of state have been graced
by my signature, but would you like to see this
masterpiece anyway?"

She nodded and watched the graceful, quietly
flowing movements of his hand as it performed a
charmingly ornate signature on a piece of pressed
paper. Below it he drew a heart, entwining their
initials like a monogram. He picked up her hand
and touched his lips to her fingertips, and her
pulse tickled through her senses. In the same
archaic, romantic script, he wrote *I would never
do anything to hurt you. Are you protected?*

She stared at the words. The pen was placed
lightly in her fingers and she wrote, blotchily,
I meant to be. But I'm not. She hoped there
was some place reserved in heaven, and perhaps
in Philip Brooks' heart, for failures with good
intentions.

The pen in his hand wrote, *Let me take care of
it. And you.*

She extended her fingers slowly, touching his
mouth. "It's a good thing one of us knows what he's
doing," she murmured. "I should have said this
before . . . you're very nice, Philip."

The humor in his eyes grabbed at her heart. "Now say to me—'and you're very sexy, Philip.'"

"And you've very—" Her throat tightened like a clamp on the words—a smile was blossoming—"*very* sexy, Philip."

"Now say 'Kiss me, Philip.'"

She could feel the suspended sexual longing in his body. "Kiss me," she breathed. His fingers separated hers, and slid between them, bringing their palms together. She was floating and frightened, flame-light, alive with her own apprehensions and need and love. Her fears had returned because it had become suddenly, blindingly real. She was waking from a dream and finding it had become her life.

His lips moved to take hers, sailing lightly against her tense lips, alternating the pattern and placement of his mouth gently, until her mouth grew receptive and tingling, opening to his potent melting kisses. His tongue stroked provocatively against hers and then he drew back to kiss her eyelids, her cheeks, her nose. His cheek rubbed hers.

His eyes closed, he brought the tips of their noses together, laying his brow upon hers, tracing his thumb over the glazing of her mouth, penetrating slightly inside.

"Jenny? Do you want to love me now? Jenny, my soft, wonderful lady—do you want us to be together?"

Sparks grew in many places inside her. Yes. She wanted him. Her body was raw with wanting, doubts were vanquished, her spirit tripping through the grass with his in a slow motion haze. What foolery of brain was this that had suddenly put these darts of vacillation into her? No. Vacillation was too strong a word; it was some form of excited apprehension that nipped at her heels. Virginal anxiety. Ugh. Unforgivable of her temperament to do this to her. At her age, this ought to be simple. Fine. She'd just ignore it. But she heard herself say,

"Phillip, I know this will sound crazy, but wouldn't a short walk be nice?" She winced internally at the nervous brightness in her voice. "We could bundle up warm and—" The words trailed and her dignity seemed to sink with them into oblivion. Help! She felt his hands leave her, but not his interest. His tender scrutiny singed her cheeks.

"Why not?" He stood and crossed the room in two long strides to take her clothes from the screen. "We'll pick up your boots in my bedroom. You can take the dress off there."

She stood in place like she'd stepped in a puddle of superglue. Superglue—wonderful stuff. One drop bonds forever. She fantasized scientists using it to put together space shuttles, skyscrapers. . . .

"Come, love . . ." His smile stroked her, his hand touched her arm, and the glue loosened and allowed her to walk beside him. The glue that held her joints seemed to have loosened too. Her knees kept wanting to buckle on the attic steps. Her heart did doubletime.

In the bedroom, he closed the door quietly behind them. Her boots were drying near the heating grate. He picked them up and then let them drop softly back to the carpet.

"There. I've picked up your boots. And we've

been for a walk. And I want you so much that my eyes hurt from looking at you."

Her pulse began to sprint. "I wonder how you stand me. I'm a basket case."

"No, Jenny." He lifted her, the gown murmuring against his legs, his face nuzzling her hair. "You just haven't learned how to pretend."

He let her down on the bed so gently she seemed to float against the bedclothes. She felt the mattress pull as he came down at her side, and his long legs stretched out next to hers. She put her face into his sweater, breathing in his sweet scent through the warm wool.

Not looking up, she said, "The part is coming, I think, when you undo my buttons with your expert fingers. So my romances have always said. I'm widely read, if not . . ." A soft ahem, ". . . experienced."

"You may have been misled." His finger tipped up her chin and trailed slowly down her cleavage. "It doesn't take much expertise to undo buttons."

Tact, perhaps, had made him bypass comment on her point. Conscientious to the end, she repeated it. "Philip—I've never had a lover before."

"No!" The sternly beautiful mouth affected shock, though there was tender laughter in his eyes. "And here I was, imagining you did this all the time."

He was on his side by her, so close that his breath anointed her skin, his fingertips drawing tingling patterns on her throat. Someone had put her smile on crooked.

"It's eerie," she said, "this process of losing my innocence."

His cheek rested on her hair. "I want to make

love to you—I'd never want to take your innocence. I want to give you things. Good things."

He curved her shoulders into his arms and covered her mouth with his, staying with her while he laid her down on her back, drawing the gown lower to bare her shoulders and the soft white curve of the top of her breasts. He pulled back and found her looking up at him, the dense burnt-honey eyes wide and bright. And petrified. And love-flushed. As an experiment, he picked up her wrist and poised it in midair. He let go and it stayed there. Her earnest expression didn't change. Hmm, he thought. This is going to take a little imagination. Inside he was melting with laughter and sympathy. He disciplined his face and observed in a soft tone, "You seem a little tense, love."

"I do?" Her chest heaved with the effort of breathing.

He reached out a forefinger to her wrist and gently pushed down the stiff arm. His hands on her waist brought her up to sit cross-legged, and he sat in front of her, their knees contacting like a current. Her breasts pushed against the delicate lace, and he imagined her softness arching into his chest while he loved her. Thoughtfully, he peeled back her gown to uncover one bare curving foot, and he ran a lazy finger along her instep.

"Do you know how screech owls mate?" he murmured, watching her face.

She shook her head.

"You've seen Chaucer. He's a screech owl—those funny little owls about the size of a beer can. You can find them all over the country." He took one of her immaculate pink toes and wiggled it affectionately. "It usually takes a male owl two or three days of studying a female from afar before he has the nerve to approach her. On the big day, he looks more and more nervous as dusk falls. He spends time making sure his feathers are just so—fluffing them up, preening them back into place. Then he'll begin to call her. It's a haunting call, melodious and a little plaintive; kind of a trill with an upward inflection at the end, like a question."

"What does the female do?"

"Looks like she wishes he'd drop dead." He touched his fingers to her lips, and then to her toes, and covered them up again. "He keeps calling, circling from a barn roof, to a fence, to an oak tree, to a hay stalk, each time closer to her. The closer he gets, the sillier he acts, bobbing his body like a jack-in-the-box, swiveling his little head. Sometimes when he lands on her branch—as far away as he can get without toppling off the limb—he'll wink at her in this comical way, one eye at a time."

She smiled, imagining Chaucer.

"By then, her expression is priceless—kind of a variation on 'what have I done to deserve this?' The more she ignores him, the more frantically he'll bob and swivel. Sometimes if he gets too close, she'll chase him away crossly, flapping her wings. Then he's crushed. He squats on the outermost edge of the limb and sinks his head way down into his fluffed breast feathers until his beak has all but disappeared, and moans disconsolately."

She knew her smile was on crooked again.

"The female either decides she doesn't want him,

and glides away into the night, or she decides she does. If she does, she'll sweep her head sideways and look right at him, and then mosey over closer to him." His body turned on the bed and he sat beside her, sidling closer, crowding her and making her laugh.

"What does the male do then?"

"Cheers right up. His eyes brighten, and his head comes up."

Her stomach tightened as he brought his hand to rub softly and beguilingly on the small of her back.

"They have very touching love play." His breath disturbed a wisp of hair, making it flutter against the inner configuration of her ear. "Sometimes they touch beaks." His mouth touched hers with light humor. "He strokes her with his beak . . . on her nape . . . shoulders . . ." His lips were following his words, making her smile, sending crisp shivers through her. "Her breast plumage . . ." Through the fabric, his mouth discovered a turgid point and he teased it to aching fullness with his tongue. "They mate for life." His breath, cooling the fibers, rushed her senses with another tumult of shivers.

His mouth left her and he lay down at her side, his length relaxed and inviting like his smile. "She can fly away any time she chooses. So can you. You see? It's natural to think about it first. It's natural to be cautious." He rolled onto his back, his blue eyes fetching, his smile sensual. "Maybe you should set the pace. What would you like to do to me?"

The luster in her eyes became a glow as she studied his face. Then she delighted him by saying,

"Hadn't you better be careful? What if it was something truly debauched?"

"I'd count my blessings. Go ahead. Debauch me."

She looked at him again, then blushed and laughed. "I want to. But you'd better hint me in the right direction."

His mouth was good-natured, his eyes full of sexual heat. "Pull up my sweater. Lay your hands on my bare chest."

Shaky but eager, her fingers pushed his sweater upward to expose his chest, and he arched his back to help her. Her fingers spread wide open over his chest, her warm palm nestled in his light, springy hair. His breath came in long slow swells, deepening at her touch. A drowsy look came into his eyes.

"Run your fingers over my skin, Jenny . . . just lightly." His eyes closed, the full sensual lids with their straight dark lashes seemed to decorate the perfection of his cheekbones. "Like that. Let your fingers wander over me."

Shy as a trespasser, she followed his chest, his throat, the angles of his jaw and face. The shyness left, drifting off, and she laid her hand on his flat muscled stomach where it lifted and lowered with his relaxed breathing. She slipped her hand lower and he stirred, his breath quickening, and she realized that he wasn't as relaxed as he looked. A strange excitement quivered through her with the knowledge. She lifted her hand again and laid it tentatively on the heat pushing against the cotton of his jeans.

He took a sharp breath, the corners of his wide mouth curling upward. "*Very* widely read."

"Body parts that change size . . ."

His eyes opened into the mischief in hers, and he gave her a thick grin. "I know. It's disgusting, but I can't help it."

"It's not disgusting," she whispered slowly, and laid her head on his lap, savoring his deep warmth through the cotton, the heat that felt so right to her. Time moved like a slow river.

"That's nice," he breathed. "Better than nice."

Her lips touched him in a light hesitant kiss that flickered upward to the sweet-tasting skin stretched tightly on his stomach, feeling it contract involuntarily. Pulses sang everywhere inside her as she glanced soft kisses up and across his chest, reaching his mouth, lowering her lips to his in a voluptuous open-mouthed kiss.

His strong hands sought her hips, raising them, pulling her to straddle him. "Come up."

The gown spread around them like a dazzling pale lily pad. Underneath, her nakedness got a warm shock as she contacted the faint roughness of the pliant fabric between her thighs. His hands on her hips, supporting her, felt its echo and the answering fire in his body. Love ran through him, a vibrant erotic babble, a demand, a plea.

Her desire pressed in her throat, inside her thighs, and she braced her palms giddily against his shoulders. His hands left her sides and slipped under the dress hem, caressing their way up her legs, inflaming the bare delicate flesh, curving over her bottom and gathering her into his hands. Gently she was pressed into him, against him, in a skillful motion that kindled a soft cry from her, and a spreading flame in her nerve centers.

"Philip—"

"I know." His head lifted. His tongue caressed the jumping pulse in her throat. His voice was soft, husky. "I understand. Alien me—vulnerable you . . . It'll be all right. It's just love. Me loving you; you loving me. That's all."

She was breathing in quick shallow exhalations, luxuriating in the slow path of his hand trailing upward, disarraying her gown so that it fell back, exposing her leg in a pretty white arc. His fingers curled and held her breast. With the barest pressure, the tip of his little finger traced the tiny crescent of areola that rimmed above the fabric.

He felt her thighs tighten convulsively around him as his hand slipped under the fabric, curving on the underside of her breast, pushing upward on the dainty heaviness. His fingertip uplifted her nipple. A rapid shudder took her, and him, and he dragged her close, one hand cupping her nape, the other the softness of her bottom so that her breasts were near his mouth.

She was like a leaf, drifting downward into heady delirium, riding the upcurrents, lightheaded and liquid in her arousal. For a spinetingling second his breath warmed her nipple; then his mouth warmed her, his tongue gently probing. Flushing everywhere with a light, odd heat, she felt his body shift and his upper thigh rose to support her fleecy nakedness, the pressure direct and coaxing.

After a swooning moment, she whispered, "If I flew away now, would you moan disconsolately?"

"I'd set records." His smile shaped against her breast. "Stay. I'll probably moan anyway."

His hands altered, bringing her mouth to his, pressing her full swollen lips into extended kisses, his tongue slipping into her in a deep hard motion. Slowly, they changed positions, their mouths remaining in tantalizing contact. He was on top of her, her sweetness brushing his body, her eyes passion-drenched and lustrous. Gasping, he pulled away, burying his head in the arch of her neck. His hair, tipped with dampness, heightened the caress on her skin.

"Do you—" He drew an unsteady breath. "Do you still want to go for a walk?"

She shook her head weakly.

His thumb made a soft shaken path across the satin wetness of her bottom lip and he watched it glisten with a shining crimson glow.

"You . . . want this . . . to happen now?"

"Yes." It hardly sounded like her voice. It was a wonderful voice, a rich, lyrical ballad of a voice. Her body was a fiery rhapsody.

He stood and shed his clothes, a simple matter-of-fact act, graceful but without art. Everything came off in a heap on the floor. She smiled.

He drew the dress gently over her hips and down, freeing her from the rippling folds. His hands, warm as sunlight, found her, and her sharp inward breath lifted her ribcage, thrusting her breasts into the exploration of his palms. His lips followed where his fingers led, his silken-gold hair was a heady caress on her hot body. He returned to her lips, concentrating his attention there, playing his tongue gently in and out of her mouth. His palm found her inner thigh and his fingers tangled smoothly in her tiny springy curls, letting the slight warm weight of them work their subtle magic, her body moving in unthinking rhythm against the heel of his hand.

His brain filled with a fire of enchantment, and he encouraged her with adoring disjointed phrases and the deepening pressure of his hand. They were drifting together in a storm of sunlight, dancing molecules, the stuff life was made of. He couldn't give her enough, pleasure her enough. His love was open and flowing to her, and he wanted to give and give. His senses registered each shiver of her body, every pulse.

She shuddered lightly, her clenched muscles resisting the slow penetration of his finger, and his breath was soft and moist, flooding the chamber of her ear.

"It'll be all right, Jenny. Let me." His tongue traced small circles on the violent pulse in her throat. His voice was a barely audible whisper. "Let it happen, Jenny. It's love . . . just love. . . . Close your eyes and let it happen."

Thought shut down for her, and she felt only the updraft of her ascent. Icy wires of feeling immersed themselves in her nerves, hot waves spun through her muscles. Her flesh blazed. Her hands submerged in his thick, soft-textured hair, and it pushed buoyantly against her fingers. Then the ascent spiraled, and her temperature pitched, plummeted, and then leaped upward in a devastating fluctuation. The sunlight came inside. . . .

He prolonged her ecstasy with kisses, nourishing it, until she came to rest beside him in a state not unlike sleep, as blank, as quiet, but conscious and sublime. Paradise. The world faded into a dream.

Presently he began to rouse her with love words and kisses. His flesh had a warm, new-cream taste to her, and carried a pungent intoxicating scent, like crushed lilac petals. Her own flesh was covered with a faint sheen of perspiration that warmed the path of his hands, making his touch ride her skin until her need became turbulent again. Her thighs had opened around one of his. Her mouth, glazed in moisture, received the thrust of his tongue. Her heartbeat thundered in her arteries, higher, harder, uneven, like his voice as it bathed her.

"Are you ready to feel me inside you, love?" His voice was soft, thick with passion.

She nodded and his hands brushed gently, shakily on her brow, soothing back her damp hair. He blew softly along her hairline, and slowly entered her.

The first sensation was pain. Her tight flesh stung and pulled, resisting him. His hand stayed on her forehead, stroking and stroking, and his hips coming against her were slow, so slow.

When he was all the way inside her, filling her completely, his whisper shivered against her moist lips. "Oh Jenny . . . oh darling . . . this feels so good. . . ."

Watching his face above her, she saw his eyes focus in a blurred way, as though the sound of his own voice woke him slightly. He smiled down at her, the wide mouth breathtakingly sensual.

"Sorry . . ." he breathed. His eyes had become hypnotically bright. "Sorry . . . that I'm not . . . not more eloquent."

Headily, she eased herself deeper around him. "One small step for man . . ."

His laughter was a ragged shiver. His tongue passed between her parted lips and played lightly along the uneven line of her teeth.

"Why do you like to do that?"

"I don't know," he murmured, pressing his lips low on her throat. "I love you. I love you." And his hands were gentle on her body, guiding her sweetly as they had in their dance, and again, together, they saw dreams.

They fell asleep in a square of white winter sunlight, cuddled like kittens under the yellow bedclothes, his love words her lullaby.

A distant sound pulled her from her sleep. In the first bewilderment of wakening, she didn't recognize it. Orientation took her a dazed moment. Philip's house. Philip's bed. The sound she'd heard had been the front door. There were footsteps on the stairs. She sat upright and looked at Philip's face, pure and blissful in sleep. The steps grew closer. Desperately, she shook him awake.

Philip wavered into consciousness in time to see Darrell bouncing through his bedroom door in a maroon sweat suit and a suede jacket slung over his shoulder. He stopped on the threshold and stared at Jennifer.

"Do I know you?" he asked, fixing her with an interested frown.

"No!" she said, and disappeared totally under the bedclothes.

Philip watched blearily as Darrell shrugged and raised a hand in greeting.

"It's one o'clock, you know," Darrell said, settling comfortably against the bedpost. "Sorry I'm a little late, but I had Bruno in to the vet for his shots and he was kind of under the weather so I took him out for a nice walk, and then I had to pick up the Corvette from the shop."

Filling up inside with pity for Jennifer, Philip sat up numbly and patted the cover over her head comfortingly. One o'clock, he thought. What have I forgotten?

"We were going to the gym to work out, remember?" Darrell prompted. "You know, run a couple of laps." He ran around the bed and back. "Pump some iron." He dropped in place and did a series of fast muscular pushups. "Then we were going to watch the Bucks and have dinner. Hey, that's okay. You forgot. No problem. I can dig it. Getting it on is important, too."

The situation was clearly beyond saving. Philip combed his hair back with his fingers, and said gently, "Jenny? This is my friend Darrell."

A terse and muffled "How do you do?" emanated from the blankets.

"Hey," Darrell demanded with an unfortunate flash of recognition. "Is that the librarian? Are you sleeping with her now?"

Philip sighed. "Jenny, do you mind if I tell Darrell I'm sleeping with you?"

"Not at all," said the hump of blankets.

Philip looked back at the six feet four inches of soft-hearted hunk who, next to Jack Campell, was his best friend in the world. "Yes, I'm sleeping with her. Darrell, I'm sorry for forgetting about this afternoon, and I don't want to seem inhospitable, but—"

"Hey, don't worry about it. It's cool. I'm glad to see you get a little action. You're always so fussy about who you make it with. . . . You want me to leave, right? Hey, really, you know I never would have come in if I knew she was here, but you've never had a chick in here before. You told me it upsets the owls. I'll come back later and we can do dinner." An alternate thought occurred to him. "Unless you don't want to have dinner either."

The tone was so plaintive that even Jenny, buried under the covers, caught the inflection. She said, "He can come to dinner."

Below the aviator sunglasses, Darrell's mouth took on a pleased grin. "Great. I'll bring wine. Happy recreation!"

Philip waited for the front door to close behind Darrell before he peeled back the sheet. His fingers touched the sleep-mussed hair back from her cheeks.

"I love you," he said.

"But do you respect me still?"

"Well, no, but—" He watched her emerge from the bedclothes in her pink loveliness to attack him with a pillow. Shaking with laughter, they twined together, tumbling against each other in a mist of joy.

"Is Bruno his German shepherd?"

"Close. His Doberman. Don't worry about Darrell. He won't have bad thoughts. No one's ever told him that sex isn't a form of aerobic exercise."

The brown eyes grew wide open as if in shock. "You mean it isn't? Bring me a mirror!"

He found one in the bathroom and brought it to her. She stared into it with avid concentration.

"Yep." She studied her eyes. "Lines of dissipation. I see them."

He ran his tongue over a crescent of freckles on her shoulder. "Those are scratches in the mirror."

"Oh. You're right. Well, anyway, now I'm a woman."

He kissed her tenderly. "All woman. How do you feel? Are you sore?"

"A little. I have the weird feeling that when I get up, I may walk like a cowboy."

He laughed and pressed a gentle kiss on the winsome curls at the base of her neck, nuzzling his face against her cheek.

She sighed. "After this, I have a feeling that the rest of my life is going to be a letdown."

"I'll spend the rest of mine making sure that doesn't happen," he whispered, and let his lips find hers.

Even then, she felt a thrill of fear. Outside, the world was waiting.

Nine

He drew a tub for her in his grandmother's bath, enjoying the way her wide-eyed gaze fell on the elaborate pink-tiled walls, the tub's pink and gold Lindspar relief, the life-sized Italian sculpture in the corner of *Venus, Surprised In Her Bath.*

Then he sat on a footstool, resting his bare arms on the tub, and watched her bathe. The scent of her skin, fragrant and steamy from the bath, rose around him like a sensual cloud. He dipped his finger in the warm water and let it wander desultorily over her throat where the faint rosiness told him that she was shy yet about having him see her body.

As she had eased herself gracefully into the bath, he had seen her wince when the sore petals of her femininity touched the water, and he was sorry. This sting of guilt he hadn't anticipated, guilt at having caused her that brief unavoidable pain, guilt at having pulled her from her safe oblivious slumber. Partly what had passed between them was the inevitable outflowing of love, natural and perfect. She was a romantic, reticent to bloom. He had sensed that in her. But also he was experienced, and not stupid. He knew he had done subtle things, some of them probably unconscious, to heighten her desire for him and to make it impossible for her, in her innocence, to fight the experience. Had he taken something from her? Choice? And, he remembered, she hadn't said it yet: *I love you.*

Chaucer, who spent a great deal of his day sleeping, came floating through the doorway, silent as a shadow, and landed on Philip's bare shoulder. Absently, he stretched up a damp hand to scratch the downy breast feathers.

"Aren't his talons sharp?" Jennifer asked.

"They're razors. He has remarkable control, though. We've had a couple of accidents that were mostly my fault, but he's never hurt me deliberately. Have you ever touched an owl feather? There's nothing softer. Owls have a downy fringe on their primary flight feathers to muffle wing sounds so they can hunt in silence. Here. Give me your hand."

Chaucer seemed to take exception to the sparkling cascade that ran from her arm as she raised it from the water. He flew off, landing on the wall mirror, knocking it askew.

"If you have an owl in the house, your pictures never hang straight," Philip said.

"Have I offended him?"

"No. He wants to watch us in the mirror. Can you see? Very sneaky, isn't he? Birds seem to love melodrama. Hmm. He's spotted the plastic soap-dish that I knocked into the water."

Jenny began to smile, watching Chaucer bend toward the mirror to eye the rectangle of white plastic that floated by her knee. Philip touched the water, the soap dish rocked wildly, and Chaucer's ear tufts went up, giving his face a hilarious expression of surprise.

"What we have here is an owl IQ test," Philip said. "What is it, Chauce? Come and see. Is it a fishie?"

Chaucer sailed to the edge of the tub and glared at the soapdish. Jenny gave the dish a little push and Chaucer's head swiveled, following the movement with poised intensity. He leaned closer and closer, his small face ludicrously fierce. Finally he lost his balance entirely, and toppled head first into the water. Philip's long graceful hand scooped up an angry sopping mess of feathers, clacking beak, and wildly flailing wings.

Laughing, his whole attention directed to the raucously chattering owl as he carefully wrapped it in a towel, he said, "Sorry, old man, you flunked. You're a bird of very little brain. Don't you want Jenny to think you're a wise old owl? This is a soap dish, not a fish."

He held the soap dish up, and Chaucer attacked it, biting and clawing it furiously.

"Oh, calm down, it didn't do a thing to you. Always such a fuss. There. Now you've put a hole in the towel. Are you satisfied?" Feeling Chaucer struggle to be released, he set the little owl on the floor and watched him trudge out the door, hunched into his damp breast feathers, trailing water. Philip turned back toward the tub. "He'll probably dry off in the sun. Nocturnal animals love to get their vitamin D from taking sunbaths. Sometimes I have the idea that—"

Her head was tipped downward. A tiny diamond of moisture twinkled like a gem at the corner of her lips. Coming quickly down on his knees beside her, he saw that it was a tear, that her eyes were filled with them. He felt his heart contract, the movement quick and mechanical like the rev of a fading generator. Afraid to know, but ill from the suspense of even this half-minute wait, he whispered, "Darling, what's the matter?" and was surprised that his voice could sound so rational, so gentle.

She put her forehead against his cheek, her hair tickling like whiskers from some small soft mammal.

She choked out, "I was thinking . . . about how wonderful you are."

The wound of his guilt healed, as though she had touched him with a sweet chaste spell.

She ate an orange in the butler's pantry, sitting on the pillow that he had given her half-laughingly, and watched him start dinner.

"What do you think the chances are of your becoming bored with me quickly?" She bit into a segment and discovered that he didn't buy seedless oranges.

"Nil."

"What if I asked you thousands of nosy questions about yourself?"

"I'd give you thousands of nosy answers. Please,

for God's sake, don't be silent. I want to know you're here. Every minute."

His words gave her a secret shiver of glee, but somehow the nosy personal questions were slow to come. Instead she said, "Do you remember having a butler?"

"Yes."

"What was he like?"

"German. Very Gothic face. His eyes looked like they could burn through the wall. He scared the pants off my mother. But he played a mean game of cribbage, and he taught me how to ride a bike in the side courtyard."

"Why do you call this the butler's pantry?"

"This was his domain. He ran the house from here. See the inner window above the maple cupboard? That's the servant's staircase just behind it. He could watch their comings and goings. Through that door," he pointed, "was the formal dining room, and there is a panel missing from the door, as you can see, so he could overhear the dinner conversation and intervene with a new course whenever it was tactful. And you can see the big board of keys hanging on the wall in the corner. Sixty keys, none of them marked. Werner knew by memory what each one was for and where it belonged on the board, so he'd be able to tell at a glance if anyone was using a key they shouldn't be. He was the only one in the house with that knowledge. My mother didn't even know. But when my father let him go, Werner taught the board to me before he left." Philip fell silent for a moment; reflective. "Now I'm the only one who knows the board. . . . It has a medieval flavor, being rich."

His tone wasn't defensive, but it was cautious.

She knew caution too well to miss it in someone else. He never talked about this. Somehow she knew. She remembered hearing Philip's friend Jack speaking late in the night—something about Philip cutting himself off. Treading warily, she said, "I've always had a soft spot for the Middle Ages. What's in that maple cupboard?"

"This one?" He set the knife on the chopping block, wiped parsley off his fingers, and swung open the cupboard door. Behind was a combination safe that looked like it meant business.

"And I was wondering where you stowed the family jewels!" she said brightly.

She was promptly and delightfully seized, her chest crushed against his. "You know what I do to women who try to tempt me into making dumb jokes about my family jewels?"

"Wildly ravish them on the kitchen table?" she suggested, her voice full of hope.

"Yes." He kissed her hard, and released her, and went back to the parsley, throwing over his shoulder, "Except when they already have a sore bottom."

She was about to give him an updated and more optimistic report on the condition of her bottom when he added, "It's a pie safe."

"What? You're kidding."

"No. It's a pie safe. When the cook made pies or whatever goodies, they were locked up in here until the butler served them."

"Those must have been some pies."

"Probably. Or they were starving the servants. It wasn't used by the time I came around. My father said it was ridiculous. He didn't like having to brave waking up the butler when he wanted to snitch pie at midnight."

"How about the big cupboard? What did they keep behind there?"

He gestured like a game show host. "Our young contestant, the lovely librarian from Emerald Lake, who, by the way, lost her virginity this morning, has chosen Door Number Three. And awaiting behind it—" he swung it open to show another vault that looked like it would have felt right at home in Fort Knox—"is the safe for the Brooks' china and Sheffield silver." He pulled the vault door open and she saw that it was empty. "The Brooks family has to start saving box tops for a new collection."

She had been raised to believe that financial matters were deeply personal, and there was something uncomfortable about asking a lover what his income was, but darn it all, this was relevant. She drew a breath that left her feeling lightheaded. "Philip," she asked, "are you rich or poor?"

There was a food cooler behind a heavily glazed window in the wall over the counter, that once had been used with huge blocks of ice during the summer months. During the winter, it was a natural refrigerator, and he pulled out a package of Emerald Lake bluegills and started to unwrap them, giving himself time to be sure he had the right words. An apology would have been an insult; softpedaling, foolish. Thank God, this part of it wouldn't make any difference to her anyway. To him, that knowledge was a luxury.

"In a list of income levels in last week's *Journal* I found mine—after taxes—under the heading

PROUD TO BE OFF WELFARE. The taxes on this place ought to be listed in Guinness."

He glanced at her and found she was watching him with friendly interest, her brown eyes peaceful. The image returned of seeing her that first night at the Club, her face among the maze of faces, her burnt honey eyes looking at him differently, as a man instead of a lab animal. He had seen the regret and disappointment come into them when he began to dance. After that, she had treated him like an enemy and he had had to open up his soul to her to show her that he was real again, a process that had not been without its terrors. Here they were together. It should be simple, and yet it wasn't. The idiocy of his job stood between them, more now than it ever had. There was nothing he could do except to anticipate grimly the moment she realized how much.

"What people think of as the great Brooks financial empire has been overextended since the Depression. There was a brief comeback during the Second World War when the railroads did pretty well hauling scrap metal, but after that things tottered for years. And my parents were . . . very gentle people, not business brains. They made the best decisions they could, but it wasn't enough." A memory surfaced, like a sharp stab, of his father sitting with him on his bed at dusk, explaining in a raw unfamiliar tone that they had failed to save his heritage for him. "To have kept it alive they would have had to love money more, and they couldn't. Lily Hill was our summer house. When I was sixteen they had to sell the house in Chicago and we moved back here permanently. They both died within three years of stress-related things. Dad had a congenital heart defect. I remember the day I came back after college and turned the key in the front door and stepped into this huge pile, knowing that I was the only person left in the world it meant anything to. When my parents died I grieved for them intensely, and then the grief left and I just seemed to shut down inside. . . ."

"Philip—I'm sorry."

He came to her, cupped her face and kissed the tip of her nose. "It was a long time ago."

"You . . . couldn't you find work as a biologist?"

"Not close enough to live here. Not that would pay enough to take care of the taxes."

"It's important for you to keep the land." She made her words a statement, and even so, saw emotion tighten in every muscle in his face.

"The land is a wildlife preserve. It's been in my family for generations. I'd sell the bones of my ancestors to a dog kennel before I'd let developers slice it up into sublots. God knows I don't want to keep it. I've been trying to give it to the state but they only want to accept it as a park. . . ." He reminded himself consciously not to leap on a soapbox. "Parks are fine. They have a place. But people don't have to have every damn acre of the earth to tramp over. Some animals adapt to public access, but many species are profoundly disturbed in the natural course of their lives—finding food, caring for their young, selecting mates. All you would have needed was one trip to Yellowstone Park ten years ago to see the bears begging at car windows like hookers." The soapbox. One more sentence; that's all you get, Brooks. He could see the distress building on her face. "Park land tends to serve people, not animals."

She was quiet for a moment before speaking. "Will state officials change their minds?"

"I hope so. It's going to be damned hard to dance my routine with arthritis."

Darrell arrived with a bouquet of daisies which he handed to her. Glancing down at the pillow she was sitting on, he asked, "Have you two been ice skating, or what?"

They were nearly finished with dinner when Philip, who had been rather dreamily watching her spread wild grape jelly on a piece of cornbread, said, "Darrell helped make the jelly."

Darrell looked pained. "Do you have to tell the world?" To Jennifer he said, "Wait until summer comes. Every damn weekend he has Jack and me out doing some damn thing like picking rhubarb, or elderberries, or raspberries, or slogging barefoot through some swamp picking cattails for flour. Then fall comes and and he has you out picking apples and canning them into applesauce."

"If you're ever marooned in the wild, you'll know how to survive." Philip laughed at Darrell's expression. "Maybe I do it for the pure joy of seeing you standing over a hot stove in your aviator sunglasses, wearing an apron over that corny muscle shirt of yours, stirring a pot with a big wooden spoon." He stood. "Can you excuse me for a minute? The bird feeder needs attention."

Men made Jennifer shy, and she couldn't change overnight. Nor had she forgotten that on one meeting with Darrell he had been naked, and on another, she had been. While they finished eating together, he tried with unexpected kindness to draw her out. She was attempting to respond, ashamed of her own stiff manner, when Chaucer arrived at a glide.

"If there's anything I hate," Darrell said glumly, "it's eating while that owl is around, fighting with you over every bite."

Chaucer landed on the table, bobbed, subjected Darrell to a scornful survey and then went to Darrell's plate. He marched up one side and down the other of Darrell's mashed potatoes, then jumped on his water glass and bent over for a sip.

Darrell's expression made her try to hold in her laughter, but it came sputtering out. She was carried away by it when Chaucer leaped on the vase to inspect a daisy and then nipped off its head. Darrell's long-suffering grimace did nothing to bank her mirth, which didn't begin to subside until she realized he was staring at her intently.

"You're real foxy when you laugh," he said.

She knew her cheeks had begun to color. "Thank you."

He smoothed over the bird tracks in his potatoes and took a bite. "You really blow Philip away, you know."

"Philip blows me away, too." Through the window she could see Philip in the snow, his lean outline defined by a backdrop of cranberry bushes, their bright red berries glowing in the weakening light. As she watched, a tiny black-capped chickadee landed on his hand and flew away with a sunflower seed. A glance at Darrell caught a subtle emotion: hero worship, deep affection.

"You know the patience it takes to make them

trust him like that?" As though it were something that struck him on impulse he asked, "You
sure you care a lot?"

"I'm sure."

"That's good. I'd hate to see him get hurt. People don't understand him. They think he's"—a
hesitation, a half-smile—"you know, like me. A
great-looking, empty-headed stud. Makes him pull
away from people. Chicks usually just want to get
in his pants. Jack is the only friend he keeps
from the old days when the family had big dough.
Jack says that's because Philip can't afford to
party in the same style anymore, and if he can't
pay for himself, he doesn't go. People from town
are bashful with him. He's a *Brooks*. Sometimes
they get this idea that he's cold because he's so
comfortable being alone. But he's not cold. This is
one sweet guy."

Those words returned to her later as she stood
beside Philip in his softly lit bedroom, watching
him put the baby owls to sleep in a wooden box.
He spoke to them in a low tone, stroking the
downy feathers soothingly, his hands graceful as
a magician's, the long-boned fingers beautiful,
clean and golden.

"I want to make love," she said softly, lifting
aside his hair to brush her mouth on the back of
his neck.

He closed the box lid and turned quickly on his
chair, a smile in the clear compelling eyes. "A
beautiful sentiment. Am I doing something to in-
spire it?"

"Watching your hands makes me want to feel
them on . . . on me."

"Show me where." His soft tone matched hers,

his gaze reaching out to her as he offered her his hands.

A sharp sensation escalated in her chest, cold and hot at one time, the keen anticipation of her body. Grasping his wrists, she guided them to her waist, stirring them against the T-shirt of his that she wore. The motion stretched the fabric, teasing it over her breasts and back. She closed her eyes and saw bright-hued streams of primary colors, felt the tingling sweetness of her awakening nipples.

His hands revolved in lazily widening circles, spreading to her hips, and in back, to the cheeks of her bottom. The world careened around her as his strong fingers framed her thighs, turning her. A flutter sank from her stomach to the warmth between her legs when his hands began to steadily caress her upper thighs. His lips touched her twice, on one back pocket, then the other, nuzzling under her T-shirt to find the margin of warm skin that bordered her jeans. The lace-work caress of his hands moved inward, and his mouth worked a deep circular motion on the small of her back as the low flutter within her became a sting.

"I love you everywhere," he murmured. She could taste his words through her skin.

She was turned again, and her hands, love heavy, found his shoulders. One of his hands dragged up the T-shirt to allow his mouth to surge over the slight convexity of her bare stomach. She began to arch into his warm mouth while it trailed over the bow of her pleasure-tightened diaphragm. His other hand went between her legs, massaging her, wringing a moan from her parted lips, and she pushed against the shelf of his palm, her blood running like hot rain.

"Do you think I'm oversexed?" she breathed into his hair, and felt it eddy against her lips, rich, like some smooth exquisite textile.

He was pulling open her jeans, slipping the zipper lower. "It's too soon to tell." The tip of his tongue followed the outline of soft curls at the base of her stomach. "But I'm hoping for the best." One of his hands climbed her ribcage, riding the impeding cloth out of the way with the back of his hand, his fingers wreathing one rampant nipple. Catching her as her knees buckled, he hauled her onto his body, sliding her thighs around his waist.

A rustle came from the wooden box on the desk. The lid popped open, rising like a hat on the fuzzy head of one baby owl, whose round yellow eyes fixed on them curiously.

Heated everywhere, desire braiding and unbraiding itself inside her body, still Jenny laughed. Philip laughed too, but she was surprised and bewitched by the breathless quality in his voice when he spoke.

"Go to sleep, you." He reached out a long forefinger and tamped the box lid down. It bounced once and then the box became quiet.

His hands, warm and large, threaded into her hair, his breath coming quickly as he pulled her into a hard kiss. Their bodies twisted feverishly together, entwined. Cradling her, he carried her to the bed. He had begun to tremble, and their hands were clumsy and fast, pulling the clothes from each other, their love an unbanked burning hunger.

"I could hardly wait—the afternoon seemed so

long. . . ." She arched her back and his mouth made a thrilling outline along the shore of her nipple.

"For me too. I tried not to—"

"What?"

"I was worried about . . ." He inhaled shakily as her mouth tripped heavy open kisses down his neck.

"About what?"

"Your poor little—Jenny, Jenny, darling, that feels like heaven."

"Poor little what?"

Laughing, his lips came into slight, moist contact with hers. "Smile. Your poor little smile." He felt it form against his lips. "Because it feels like someone's connected it right to my heart."

Philip's voice roused her in the sweet deepness of the night and she woke to find him raised up on his elbow, trying with enchanting absurdity to reason with the two tiny owlets who sat on his pillow in a spill of silver moonlight.

She lifted her head groggily. "Philip? What do they want?"

"Embarrassed as I am to admit it, they've developed this terrible habit of wanting to crawl under the covers with me."

"I can understand why," she said, laughing huskily and yawning. "Do they really sleep with you?"

He sighed and laid his head back.

"Aren't you afraid of rolling on them?"

"No. I don't move very much in my sleep. The trouble is, they don't sleep as much as they used to when I first brought them home. They chase each other around under the covers and fight. Watch this." He lifted the bedclothes. The babies skedaddled underneath, and two lumps ran around in random patterns. Finally they converged, and there was a loud clacking and frantic wing-flapping. He pulled the small furies out and separated them. Each clung to an index finger, their wings spread menacingly. One suddenly leaped into the air and landed talons down on a Kleenex box on the bedside table and began energetically ripping it to shreds.

"Okay, you two, it's the toy box for you."

"You have a toy box for them?" she wondered sleepily. "What kind of toys do owls like?"

"I have kind of a playpen for them in a bathroom down the hall. They've got an old hairbrush, mice made out of upholstery scraps, plastic balls, baby rattles. . . ."

He took care of his tiny nuisances and returned to the bedroom to find that she'd pushed the bed clear of covers. She lay in the center of the bed on her stomach, her bare legs deliciously long, her chin supported on one palm.

"How's your smile?" he asked softly, and sat down on the bed at her side.

She rolled on her back and showed him. As the breath began to catch in a hard knot in his throat, he realized that it was no bad thing to have two tiny owls that woke one up at two o'clock in the morning.

Ten

In the week that followed they spent mornings together, and called them undates. Memories collected in her mind like intimate postcards: Philip in the snowy woods kissing her brow under the tapping golden brown leaves that clung to an oak; Philip running through the genteelly fading opulence of a long hallway trailing a child's pulltoy—Buzzy Bee—with Chaucer chasing excitedly. Philip drawing her back from a daydream by touching the glossy softness of an owl feather slowly under the curve of her bare knee.

A raft of rumpled stationery grew in her wastebasket, each with a few lines on it that read,

> Dear Mom,
> I'm in love! His name is Philip and he's a—

Or they read,

Dear Mom,

It's happened, I've met *him*. It's wonderful and I'm still reeling. His name is Philip and he's a––

Sometimes she could laugh about it. Sometimes she could not. Her mind retreated from the thing he did when they were apart, shunning it like a bad neighbor. She deceived herself that she was tolerant. She had a constant heart-in-the-throat feeling, an elated teetering happiness. At moments, she felt the strong need to share the richness of it, the hidden burning problems with another human being, a wise objective source; but she wasn't in the habit of making those sorts of confidences. It was difficult enough for her to divulge a single constrained statement to Annette. They were alone in the break room in Friday's quiet, sipping coffee.

"I spent the weekend with Philip," Jenny said suddenly, and waited.

Annette set down her mug and studied Jenny with fascination and empathy, and grinned. "You lucky duck. I'll bet every moment was golden."

"Most of them were."

"Well, you know what? He's a lucky duck, too."

Jennifer was alone on Friday night, closing up the library, damping down the image of Philip at work. Muted shadows hung like soft shrouds from the stacks. Leaves from the green hanging plants gleamed in the iridescent varnish of the security lights.

She heard a knock at the back door and ran to answer it, wishing that some miracle had happened and it would be Philip. It had. It was. She was in his arms immediately, her warm body pleasantly cooled by the wintry radiance from his jacket as his arms enfolded her. His mouth was soft, his cheeks windslapped and chilled, innocently rosy. Even on a winter night his hair carried the fragrance of sunshine. She tried to pull back to see him better, but he held her close, almost desperately so.

She sighed against his lips. "I'm sorry, sir, the library's closed. You'll have to use the after-hours depository."

"I could," he murmured, "but it just wouldn't be the same." His face nestled in her hair, moving from side to side, allowing it to polish his face. "This morning was a century away. Will you adopt me? Keep me in a box by your bed?"

"Anything." As his fingers followed the ridge of her spine down, she moved restlessly. "*Anything.* I thought you had to work tonight?"

He drew back then, his muscles subtly tightening. "There was some kind of weird feedback in the sound system so they had to cancel the first show. I have to go in later." One arm left her shoulder and he held up a gaily ribboned present. "I brought you something."

She opened it there in the hall. It contained a child-sized overnight bag with the cheerful lettering "Going To Grandma's!"

"Pack that when you stay the weekends with me and no one will suspect a thing," he said. She made a wry face at him and began to laugh, flushing helplessly.

"It's very elegant."

"I shoplift only in the best departments." A gentle finger tapped up her chin for another kiss. "Are you alone?"

"Except for Jinx."

He slid an arm around her waist and began to walk with her back into the warm cavity of the library. "Yes? Let's put him back down your blouse and see what we can come up with." His arm squeezed her waist but the light tease was spoken almost absently. He released her and she watched him wander around the room, his hand straying over the walnut card catalogue, spinning the globe in the children's section, his movements restive, unaware. Finally, he dropped his jacket onto the floor and lowered his body in an attractive way onto one of the sizable floor cushions in a secluded corner. "568—Dinosaurs. Right?"

She recognized the Dewey decimal number. "Right." The careless, elegant drape of his body caught in her imagination. "You must have read dinosaur books voraciously as a kid."

"Voraciously," he said, his eyes coming alight in a way that sent burning signals through her nerves. "You have a wonderful occupation, passing on the wonderful classic books we read as kids, telling them about Winnie the Pooh—" He patted his lap invitingly.

Some part of her was beginning to sense an inner desperation under the play, and she stood paralyzed, trying to guess, to understand. But thought sank in her mind, as though the buoyance of her love was too ethereal to support fear. The air around her seemed thin and light, her limbs weightless, her heartbeat jumpy and volatile. She saw his lips curve into a smile and he came to her and drew her down beside him.

"I love you," he said, gazing into the brown eyes that had grown solemn and misty. He stroked back her bangs, uncovering her lovely brow, wanting suddenly to see her whole face. There wasn't a way to tell her. The words would be unbearable said aloud—that the sea of faces, the eager mouths that weren't hers had begun to strip some unarmored layer of his soul. The intangible cord that joined him to her neither numbed nor severed when he stepped on stage.

Needing her, attempting lightness, he let his hand slip up her sweater and watched her eyes widen and warm when he uncovered her breast. "What's this—what's your sweater made of?"

She swallowed hard. "Angora."

"Angora." He repeated the word as though it were some womanly mystery. "It's soft. But not as soft as your mouth." His lips dipped to hers and their pulses quickened together, their breathing beginning to race.

"I miss you when we're apart." He touched her upper lip with the tip of his tongue. "I've never needed anyone or anything this much. Promise you won't disappear. . . ."

"Yes," she said in a breathless whisper as his fingers laid gently over her nipple. "Philip—this is the library. We shouldn't—"

The urgency of his kiss exploded her protests. His hand slid past her knee, yearned against her stockings, sending a frazzle of shivers through her, climbing upward on her thigh. She soothed her body closer, still trying to tell him no.

"Why not, Jenny? Would it be bad . . . shocking?"

She made an attempt to nod, her eyes sparkling with passion, her lips seductively parted and dewed from his kiss.

"Then be bad for me, Jenny. I want you to

remember me here, when you're being so good and helpful and conscientious. I want you to remember this—and this—and think about me." Their kiss became wild, delicious, their hands searching each other with tender hunger. "Libraries . . . are magic places. Make magic happen for me, Jenny. . . ."

Later she walked into her apartment and thought, If anyone saw me like this, they'd know. She flumped down on her sofa, sinking into the cushions, the happy goofy smile still in place. And sighed contentedly.

"I love you, Philip Brooks," she said aloud. After a moment she began to sort through her mail with limp, pleasure-weakened fingers, letting unwanted envelopes fall like withered leaves onto the carpet after a cursory glance at the return address.

The last was from her mother and she opened it and read it and the smile faded, forgotten, gone. She touched her fist agitatedly to her forehead, and then to her mouth.

Her mother had tried to phone during the week but never caught her at home. She planned to come to Emerald Lake on Friday night—tonight, oh, God, that was tonight—with a group of friends from work. They were coming to the Cougar Club on Jenny's recommendation to see the handsomest man in the world take off his clothes. They probably wouldn't make it until the third show; Jenny shouldn't wait up. They could spend Saturday and Sunday together and wasn't it going to be great. . . .

Jenny sat on the couch, staring into space, and

realized that at last she had met herself at the blind corner of her own contradictions.

Her mother wasn't here yet.

The Cougar Club was crowded, smoky, and festive, nearing the end of the second show. Jenny sat in the shadow of a pillar, alone with her agony. Bloodless and inanimate, deaf to the ecstatic screams around her that were urging her lover to uncover his stunning body, she watched Philip strip.

He was dancing to a Sister Sledge song, the athletic grace of his body released in a sensuous flood that arrived dead-center inside each beat. His shining, light-rinsed hair moved and swirled with him. She knew intimately the precise relationship that body had with rhythm. She had learned its accuracy in love. She could feel it still, against her own.

He didn't see her, and that was probably merciful for both of them. Several times he almost seemed to look right at her, but closer study warned her that it was only a well-conceived illusion. He made no direct eye contact while he danced, or while he kissed, or while neat fingers tucked folded dollars into his G-string.

It was, finally, the kisses that were the real exercise in masochism. Visually they made a beautiful, arousing picture, the women in a series coming into Philip's arms, their clothes bright as butterflies against his golden flesh. She saw what she had missed on her first night here—how stylized these kisses were, how shorn of emotion. He smiled like an actor, the muscles accurately aligned, the eyes polite, the soul absent. Knowing that helped nothing. This was her lover, her lover's mouth, and every glamorous ritualistic kiss struck at her until she felt ill, violated, boiling in ugly inner emotion.

I must have been insane to come. Why am I here?

She jumped when firm fingers gripped her arm, and like an angry echo of her thoughts, she heard someone say,

"What are you doing here?"

She glanced up into Darrell's dark liquid eyes. For once he was without his glasses. Knowing it was childish, not caring, she snapped, "It's a free country."

"The last thing he needs is to see you sitting here with that look on your face."

She wondered indifferently what look was on her face. Stubborn in her trauma, she said, "I've paid fifteen dollars to see the show and I'm going to watch it to the end."

Darrell whirled and left her, returning soon with a handful of bills, cramming them into her purse. "Okay. I've refunded your damned fifteen dollars. Go home, Jenny."

"Sorry. I want to see the man's body."

"The man'll drop his pants for you any time of the day or night and you know it."

"For me and everyone else in the whole world with fifteen bucks."

"Keep your voice down, will you? This is a public place and I can evict anyone creating a disturbance."

"There isn't any disturbance."

"No," he said grimly, "but there will be if he sees you here with your face full of tears."

She hadn't realized, and wiped them savagely away as he pulled her through the crowd, past the bold curious stares, out a door behind the bar into a bleak quiet hallway painted a strange pastel color.

"Is this your bed of nails?" he asked, his voice quite gentle. "Go home."

"I have to talk to Philip."

"Tomorrow."

"Tonight. Now. I mean, whenever he's finished."

"Look, he wouldn't want you to see him like this. Do yourself and him a favor: go home. If you do, I'll tell him to call you the minute he gets backstage, all right?"

She detected an extra inflection in his voice. "What do you mean, see him *like this*?"

"He's been drinking," Darrell said tightly. "It's been hard for him to work since last weekend, and you know damn well why."

She grew colder and colder, her blood receding to her extremities in the same way it had when she was wandering aimlessly, freezing, the process slow and violent.

Acknowledging defeat with an exasperated breath, Darrell opened a door for her and motioned her inside. She saw two chairs, a table, a shower, Philip's clothes—the ones she'd seen leave his body when they made love in the library—a half empty bottle of Jim Beam beside a glass. On one wall was a poster of the earth, the picture taken from a satellite, a majestic deep-blue planet, cloud-hung and delicate, frighteningly reduced by distance.

A moment or two passed. Then Darrell said,

"Just remember that whatever you say tonight, you're going to have to live with in the morning."

He left. Jenny heard his footsteps stop in the hall, and his voice, speaking to someone she couldn't see.

"Sorry, man," Darrell said.

"What for?" Philip's voice reached her, his words absent and distracted, and then he appeared in the doorway, wiping his face with a towel, clad only in zipped but unsnapped jeans, one thin gold chain glittering around his neck, another draped around his ankle. Seeing her made him halt there, the towel poised at his temple where his champagne-colored hair curled damply. His blue eyes seemed to burn like lasers. Beyond that, his high-boned face was stark, expressionless. It altered, beginning to fill with emotion, and he came toward her, tossing away the towel.

He hadn't stopped to question her presence. He simply rejoiced in it. After the many numb years he was in love, a love that felt like an open wound when his mouth met with any other lips than hers. There were many raw places all over the inside of him, and in this strained and vulnerable state, her body promised sanctuary. Hazy with need, unthinking, he just tried to take her in his arms.

"Jenny?" he asked, pulling her to him.

Another time his emotion would have sliced straight to her heart. Tonight he was shellacked in perspiration that made the sinews of his muscles glisten with erotic decadence. The pure fresh fragrance she associated with his body was gone, and the heavy scents of tobacco and a hundred different perfumes clung to his skin, touching her before he did. His lips were soft and swollen, love-bitten, graphically moist. The fallen angel . . . When his mouth sought hers, her hands resisted him, her head twisting sharply away, the gesture reflexive, a creation of instinct.

Her revulsion entered his brain as though it had been injected there. There was a moment of clement inner quiet, his emotions flattening to a perfect blank, the even pitch of a radio station testing an emergency frequency. His arms slid from her shoulders.

A warm liquid sensation trickled onto his hip bone. Looking down, he found a thin red slice in his skin that had begun to bleed. Vaguely grateful for the opportunity for movement, he wet a washcloth in the shower and pressed it over the scratch.

"Another paper cut. Brand new dollar bills are fierce," he said, filling the frozen pause with empty words. Like a breath of electricity from a distant thunderhead, he felt the whispering advent of the coming pain from her rejection before it actually struck. And then it arrived, rising along his nerves like hoarfrost. Welts seemed to lift on his psyche, and he had to concentrate all his effort inward, trying to stem the glutted spill of self-hatred. He began to back away from her, registering her in his heart—the short tidy hair, her clean fingernails, the long immaculate eyelashes, each separate and satiny . . . fragile mouth, fragile eyes. Neat, bright, fastidious you, he thought; soiled me.

He sat down and listened in a remote way to the clatter of the Jim Beam bottle against the glass as he splashed it full of whiskey and swallowed it rapidly. Jenny was watching him with something akin to horror. Thankfully, the liquor seemed to compose him.

"I knew this was going to happen," he said. "But I thought it would take at least a couple of months. That's one of the things about you that I've always marveled at—I could never anticipate your timetable." He held up the empty glass. "Want to get drunk with me?"

Bruises seemed to darken behind her eyes from the pain of holding back her tears. "Philip, my mother's coming to the show tonight."

Three seconds of the perfect blank again. Then he began to laugh. It was a horrible angry sound and he stopped it as quickly as he was able to. "I'll have to pull out all the stops then. Don't worry. It's going to be wonderful. I'll make it my personal responsibility to make sure every female in the house has a fifteen-dollar climax."

"Look—" Her voice broke. "I tried to tell you this wasn't going to work. I'm too insecure. I'll drive us both insane."

"So. In the end it comes back to shame."

"Do you think this is something I feel by choice? Tell me what to do with it then."

He shot out of the chair, his hand gripping her upper arm, and turned her to face his wall poster.

"Look at it, Jenny. Do you recognize it? It's the fragile, finite Spaceship Earth. Our home. The only home we'll ever have, this lovely tiny ball hurtling through space. We can't leave it. But every year we exhaust more of our natural resources. We dump more poison into the air and water. We bury more land under concrete. Creatures that have existed on earth for millennia are dying. The delicate, elaborate ecosystem is being depleted. The earth can't feel its own future; and I can't save it. I can't save it, Jenny. Please. Please. Let me save just one little piece!"

Silence vibrated between them.

"What do I say?" Jenny's heart thumped jarringly with stress. "You're trying to save vanishing wildlife habitats. That's important. I'm trying to close off your most viable source of income so I'm small and petty and vain. Where does that leave the two of us?"

"Jenny—" The anguish inside was becoming evident in his voice. "Jenny. Love. What am I but a collection of bones and tissue, and if people want to pay money to look at that, what does it matter?"

Tears brimmed. She slashed at them with her hand. "Would you mind if I slept with another man?"

He swore softly.

She pursued it with distressed insistence. "How would it make you feel if I slept with another man?"

A pause. "Not good."

"Why? I'm just a collection of bones and tissue, and if someone else wants to make love to that, what does it matter?"

He set the glass on the table more heavily than he had intended. Jenny jumped.

"Well," he said. "That impaled me, didn't it? Hoist by my own petard. What the hell is a petard anyway?" He took a hard breath. "I'm not sure you can compare making love with nude dancing."

Looking at him became too painful. She turned, staring at the wall. "How convenient it must be, not being sure. It lets you skip off toward the blue horizon, leaving me alone with the guilt."

His hands sought her shoulders. "Jennifer, listen to me. I opened my life to you." Each word arrived with individual urgency. "It's been years since I've done that for a woman."

She began to shake. "Philip, I love you. But it hurts too much."

He tried to turn her, but she stood rigidly, not allowing it. In the end, he gave up.

"Don't love me then," he said. "You want me, you desire me, then use me. If you've started to love me and it hurts too much, then stop loving me and use me instead. Let me worry about the love. Whatever you do, *stay in my life!*"

"Philip . . ." Overwhelmed by what was happening between them, terrified by it, she tried to think, but her brain was an icy sphere, working sluggishly. A sharp involuntary movement clenched in her muscles, and his hands left her shoulders as though he interpreted it as a rejection.

"Get rid of your guilt and use me." His voice came to her from farther away. "Use me. I understand it. It's been happening all my life. Do you know how old I was when I had my first experience with a woman? Thirteen. Not a sophisticated thirteen either. I was a very sheltered kid. For God's sake, at thirteen I was still carrying frogs around in my pockets. One of my mother's friends seduced me in the hayloft of her stables and I learned everything I ever needed to know about having someone make love to you as if you were an object. Lately, of course, they want me to do a private striptease first. . . ."

Nausea slammed him in the stomach. That was

about the last thing he had intended to say to her. The last thing . . . He wondered if he was drunk. His body tolerated alcohol poorly, and he drank rarely. She should not be here, not now. This time when he turned her around, she permitted it and he discovered that she was weeping soundlessly. He fought down the urge to take her in his arms, because in his current state of mind, he wasn't sure what he might do if she pushed him away again. Instead he took her coat from her arm, slid it on her, and buttoned it, arranging the muffler he had given her carefully around her neck.

"Keep warm," he said. There was another inner struggle as the tenderness and anxious love within him begged to hold and stroke and cherish her. Then he whispered, "I genuflect to your purity, Jenny. It's just too late for me to catch up. Go on home. I won't strip in front of your mother."

She began to walk toward the door, because she didn't know what else to do. She was halfway down the hall before she heard him say, "So long. It's been swell."

Jenny walked in the front door of her apartment and found her mother sitting on the couch, wearing the green velour bathrobe that Jenny had given her for Christmas two years ago.

"Jenny!"

There she was, in the fifteen extra motherly pounds she'd never bothered to lose; the funny whimsical face, breezy brown hair and Betty Boop eyes of the woman who had kept and raised a baby girl born out of wedlock in a time and place where it had been an act of outstanding courage to do so; the woman who had worked nights to go to college and graduate school; and gone on to become an economics professor and now a speech-writer for the governor. Jenny fell into her mother's arms and felt the warmth of green velour enclose her.

"I know I'm trespassing," said her mother, rocking her back and forth, "but I told the manager I was your mother and he let me in. I had the girls drop me off here because I couldn't wait another day to see you. When you get to be my age—"

"Your age! Forty-one!"

"When you get to be my age," her mother repeated firmly, "you'd rather see your one and only child than the handsomest man in the world. Besides, if I went to see these young Cougars, Bill might get jealous." Bill was her boyfriend. "He said, why go out for steak when you can have hamburger at home? And I said, especially when all they do is bring it out, let you have a whiff of it and take it back to the kitchen! So here I am. Now. Are you going to tell me what's wrong or am I going to have to beat it out of you?"

So Jenny began to talk, and went on talking through two cups of rosehips tea and one-third of a small Kleenex box. When she was finished there was a long, long silence, before her mother spoke.

"The outer beauty we can discount, since we both know that's fun but hollow stuff. Philip Brooks sounds like he's beautiful where it really counts."

Jennifer threw a handful of tissue roses into the waste basket, rubbed her pink nose, and said thickly, "And I've been thinking too, where am I ever going to find another man with an owl?"

"Or a chicken? I take it you're going out again tonight?"

Jennifer stood up and smiled.

The forest was a quiltwork pattern of silver and slate, fragrant with the damp essence of thawing ice. Water dripped in hidden thickets. Black crystal grass rose in bent fingers from the syrupy slush under Jenny's boots.

She found Philip alone in the raccoon clearing. He was sitting on the heavy limb of a gnarled oak about eight feet off the ground. One knee was pulled up, his arm resting there, his head tipped elegantly back as he gazed upward at a sky full of gauzy clouds and bright stars.

She stood beneath the limb, shoved her hands into her pockets, and said, "It's a small bomb or firecracker."

Not a muscle twitched in his lean lengthy frame, but she felt his entire awareness homing toward her like a rocket.

"What?"

Patiently, she said, "A petard. It's a small bomb. They were used in the Middle Ages to blow holes in castles. The guy who took care of the petard was the petardeer. So I assume that someone who was 'hoist by his own petard' was blown up with his own gunpowder, or something." He had continued to sit absolutely still, almost as though he were afraid that any sudden motion of his would startle her into flight. "I went home and looked it up. I didn't want you to go through life not knowing."

"Well." There was an uncertain pause. His caution tore at her heart. "It's nice to know." He leaned down to look at her face. Then, in a confidential tone, he said, "This is a two-passenger limb."

"You think I could get up there?" she asked doubtfully.

"Leave it to my expert fingers."

She did. No sooner was she beside him, tottering uncertainly, the cold moist bark pressing into her, than she was seized in his arms and kissed with the ruthlessness and abandon she associated with historical novels that had pirates in them. Blood rushed to every place in her body that he had taught to feel pleasure. At last he withdrew enough from her so that he could look into her eyes. He was gazing at her as if he couldn't believe she was really in his arms. His gloves came on either side of her face, stroking her cheeks, molding to the curves. His eyes were radiant with love, and she found it dizzying to gaze into them.

"I figure it this way," she said. "You can't save the whole world, and I can't save the whole world, but maybe together we can save twice as much of it."

"Is that what you want to do, Jenny? Save the world with me?"

"It's one of the things I want to do with you."

His thumb slowly followed the outer ridge of her lips. "What are the others?"

She put her hands on his throat and mock-choked him, nearly spilling them both off the limb. "That!"

Lovingly steadying her, he said, "What was that for?"

"The '*it's been swell*'!"

He laughed and pulled her close again. "It *has* been swell." He nibbled at the soft skin below her earlobe, his breath sending a warm lift of pleasure down her back. "Can you forgive me for the crazy way I talked tonight? I don't want to change the woman I fell in love with because she doesn't want me to strip."

"I don't want to change the man who hand-feeds wild birds and grows parsley in a clay pot on his kitchen window ledge." She closed her eyes and pressed her lips to his thumb. "I love you."

"I love you too." His mouth replaced his thumb on her lips. Softly withdrawing, he said, "I quit my job."

Her eyes opened.

"There wasn't anything else I could do. It became untenable to go from you to so many." He gave her a lingering kiss. "This is sacred, right?"

Worry, because she was a worrier, began to kick up its heels inside her. "Right. But if you are no longer to be the smile in a lady's eyes that her husband doesn't understand . . ." She saw him smile. "Where are we going to get the money to pay the taxes on this land until we can get the state to accept it as a wildlife sanctuary?"

Her use of the word "we" delighted him so much he had to kiss her again. "We have a couple of options. I've been dragging my heels about it, but we could do pretty well selling some of the things I have in the attic."

"No!" she cried involuntarily.

"Then there's a walnut carving on the hanky-panky porch that I understand is fairly valuable, and if we could figure out how to detach it—"

"Hanky-panky porch?"

"That's what the servants used to call it. The porch that connects the guest bedrooms."

"Heavens! You decadent aristocrats. Good thing we're going to be poor. What else is on our option board?"

"There's Carrera marble in the fireplaces. Copper in the plumbing. If worse comes to worse, Jack is always trying to give me money, so maybe we could borrow some from him. And I have an uncle who would dearly love to make me some kind of an executive with his company, although that would entail us moving to Los Angeles and—I beg your pardon?"

"I said, oh dear."

He began to laugh. "You're going to be worse about these things than I am. Do you know what I was going to do?"

His kisses were making a tantalizing caress on the underside of her throat. Thought fled. "Hmm?"

"I was going to come to see you at dawn," he whispered softly, "when your resistance would be weak."

"My resistance to you is always weak." Her mouth searched for and found his, and it was ticklish for them both to balance on the limb with their arms around each other and their lips clinging and parting. But somehow they found a way.

Eleven

Jenny's hair was shoulder length now. Philip watched it lift in the sea breeze that tossed the hem of her linen dress and set rippling green grass in a caress against her bare feet and legs. Sitting on the hill above him, she was gazing toward the water where the wind-ruffled waves came in scythes to the island beach. Above, the sun shone with dazzling brilliance in a huge sky. Below the rocky promontory into the Atlantic, their launch with the logo of the Thoreau Society bobbed in the small cove.

It had taken a year to happen—to get the state of Wisconsin to accept Lily Hill as a wildlife preserve with no commercial exploitation, forever, guaranteed. A nonprofit organization dedicated to the preservation of historic buildings had taken over the mansion, and tourists walked in the restful paths and quiet corridors he had known as a child. It didn't feel as bad to him as he had thought it might. It had been a year of frantic fundraising, and of compromise, and of having to turn to others for help, which had not been easy for him. Now it was over. He and Jenny had emerged from it penniless, and so rich in their growing love that they barely noticed.

His new job with the Thoreau Society had brought them to the coast of Maine, where he was heading a project to reestablish a healthy ecology on this chain of beautiful rocky islands stretching into the Atlantic.

One of his pet programs was the return of the puffins, small roly-poly black and white birds with an oversized crescent of a beak, extinct on the islands for a hundred years. Jenny said they looked like a cross between a penguin and a duck. He had arranged to have newly hatched puffins transported here from Newfoundland, a thousand miles to the north. Now the baby puffins resided in tiny burrows that he had hand dug for them. It was his hope that when they grew old enough to migrate, they would return here to rear their young and the colony would grow and flourish, and another piece of the earth would be reborn.

He watched a tiny bump of gray fluff emerge from a burrow and snatch the bit of fish he had left there, and smiled.

He, Jenny, Chaucer, and Henrietta the chicken had found a cottage in a small coastal village, and wonder of wonders, it had a moribund library that was crying out for Jenny. With admiration, he remembered the way she'd gotten the village board to appoint her library director and had used her newfound fundraising skills to reopen it. Since then the library had become a fresh heartbeat in the village, and she'd been able to launch into a spectrum of related activities—organizing cooperative babysitting for new parents, starting a scholarship search, beginning a program of home book delivery for the elderly.

He saw Jenny wave at him, and he waved back, and then the urge overtook him to be with her. He stood up, brushing the grass and sand from his jeans, and began to run up the breezy hillside.

Jenny watched him come to her, savoring the firm wide lips, the sensitive emotions that came there, and his eyes, the bluest she had ever seen. When he reached her, their hands joined for a moment, their wedding bands glinting in the sunshine, and then he slid down beside her on the blanket, drawing her onto his lap. His fingers spread, curving around the slight swell of her expanding tummy.

"How's McFetus?" he asked.

"Perfect. But if you don't stop calling your barely begotten child by that ridiculous nickname I'm going to get my front tooth capped."

He laughed. "Oh, please. Anything but that." He bent to graze a kiss where his hand had been. "I love you, McFetus," he whispered.

She settled back in his arms, peace flowing like a tranquil stream through her. "One very nice thing about being married to a biologist is that the odder the things my body does in this condition, the more it fascinates you."

He smiled, his arms tightening around her, feeling her cheek against his heartbeat. For a long time they sat, just so, and he thought about desire, and how it had once been no more to him than a series of biological signals that could be caught and analyzed. This was a much greater thing. Immensely greater. Love.

"How can they call this chemistry?" he asked, softly. "I've never seen it in a test tube . . . captured it in an equation."

He laid her back against the blanket with infinite gentleness and Jenny experienced again a kiss from the only man ever to match her fantasies.

"Naturally your body fascinates me," he said, blowing lightly along the curve of her ear. "Did you ever think about what a lovely amazing creation it is? Think of all the sensitive nerve endings carrying messages from your skin to your brain. In your face, for example"—his finger began to follow the path of his breath—"you have the trigeminal nerve. It has three branches. One . . . transmits impulses from your forehead." He brushed a sensuous kiss there. "And from your eyelids." His lips touched her eyelids with utmost care. "Another carries impulses from your upper lip." He ran the tip of his tongue across her lip and the uneven line of her teeth. "The third . . . from your lower lip." He traced his finger delicately there, and stroked a line of kisses down her throat, past the hollow at the base of her neck between her breasts. "Do you have any idea how many sensory receptors there are in your body?"

"No," she whispered breathlessly, in a cloud of rapture.

"Neither do I." He gave her a lazy smile. "But I'm going to find every one of them."

THE EDITOR'S CORNER

For the best in summertime reading, look no further than the six superb LOVESWEPTs coming your way. As temperatures soar, what better way is there to escape from it all than by enjoying these upcoming love stories?

Barbara Boswell's newest LOVESWEPT is guaranteed to sweep you away into the marvelous world of high romance. A hell raiser from the wrong side of the tracks, Caleb Strong is back, and no red-blooded woman can blame Cheyenne Whitney Merit for giving in to his STRONG TEMPTATION, LOVESWEPT #486. The bad boy who left town years ago has grown into one virile hunk, and his hot, hungry kisses make "good girl" Cheyenne go wild with longing. But just as Caleb burns with desire for Cheyenne, so is he consumed by the need for revenge. And only her tender, healing love can drive away the darkness that threatens their fragile bond. A dramatic, thrilling story that's sensuously charged with unlimited passion.

The hero and heroine in SIZZLE by Marcia Evanick, LOVESWEPT #487, make the most unlikely couple you'll ever meet, but as Eben James and Summer Hudson find out, differences add spice to life . . . and love. Eben keeps his feet firmly planted in the ground, so when he discovers his golden-haired neighbor believes in a legendary sea monster, he's sure the gods are playing a joke on him. But there's nothing laughable about the excitement that crackles on the air whenever their gazes meet. Throwing caution to the wind, he woos Summer, and their courtship, at once uproarious and touching, will have you believing in the sheer magic of romance.

Welcome back Joan J. Domning, who presents the stormy tale of love lost, then regained, in RAINY DAY MAN, LOVESWEPT #488. Shane Halloran was trouble with a capital *T* when Merle Pierce fell hard for him in high school, but she never believed the sexy daredevil would abandon her. She devoted herself to her teenage advice column and tried to forget the man who ruined her for others. Now, more than twenty years later, fate intervenes, and Shane learns a truth Merle would have done anything to hide from him. Tempers flare but are doused in the sea of their long-suppressed passion for each other. Rest assured that all is forgiven between these two when the happy ending comes!

With her spellbinding sensuality, well-loved author Helen Mittermeyer captures A MOMENT IN TIME, LOVESWEPT #489. Hawk Dyhart acts like the consummate hero when he bravely rushes into the ocean to save a swimmer from a shark. Never mind that the shark turns out to be a diving flag and the swimmer an astonishingly beautiful woman who's furious at being rescued. Bahira Massoud is a magnificently exotic creature that Hawk must possess, but Bahira knows too well the danger of surrendering to a master of seduction. Still, she aches to taste the desire that Hawk arouses in her, and Hawk must walk a fine line to capture this sea goddess in his arms. Stunning and breathtaking, this is a romance you can't let yourself miss.

Let Victoria Leigh tantalize you with LITTLE SECRETS, LOVESWEPT #490. Ex-spy turned successful novelist I. J. Carlson drives Cassandra Lockland mad with his mocking glances and wicked come-ons. How could she be attracted to a man who provokes her each time they meet? Carlson sees the fire beneath her cool facade and stokes it with kisses that transform the love scenes in his books into sizzling reality. Once he breaches her defenses and uncovers her hidden fears, he sets out on a glorious campaign to win her trust. Will she be brave enough to face the risk of loving again? You'll be thoroughly mesmerized by this gem of a book.

Mary Kay McComas certainly lands her hero and heroine in a comedy of errors in ASKING FOR TROUBLE, LOVESWEPT #491. It all starts when Sydney Wiesman chooses Tom Ghorman from the contestants offered by the television show *Electra-Love*. He's smart, romantic, funny—the perfect man for the perfect date—but their evening together is filled with one disaster after another. Tom courageously sees them through each time trouble intervenes, but he knows this woman of his dreams can never accept the one thing in his life he can't change. Sydney must leave the safe and boring path to find the greatest adventure of all—a future with Tom. Don't miss this delectable treat.

FANFARE presents four truly spectacular books in women's popular fiction next month. Ask your bookseller for TEXAS! CHASE, the next sizzling novel in the TEXAS! trilogy by bestselling author Sandra Brown, THE MATCHMAKER by critically acclaimed Kay Hooper, RAINBOW by the very talented Patricia Potter, and FOLLOW THE SUN by ever-popular Deborah Smith.

Enjoy the summer with perfect reading from LOVESWEPT and FANFARE!

With every good wish,

Carolyn Nichols

Carolyn Nichols
Editor
LOVESWEPT
Bantam Books
666 Fifth Avenue
New York, NY 10103

THE LATEST IN BOOKS
AND AUDIO CASSETTES

Paperbacks

☐	28671	**NOBODY'S FAULT** Nancy Holmes	$5.95
☐	28412	**A SEASON OF SWANS** Celeste De Blasis	$5.95
☐	28354	**SEDUCTION** Amanda Quick	$4.50
☐	28594	**SURRENDER** Amanda Quick	$4.50
☐	28435	**WORLD OF DIFFERENCE** Leonia Blair	$5.95
☐	28416	**RIGHTFULLY MINE** Doris Mortman	$5.95
☐	27032	**FIRST BORN** Doris Mortman	$4.95
☐	27283	**BRAZEN VIRTUE** Nora Roberts	$4.50
☐	27891	**PEOPLE LIKE US** Dominick Dunne	$4.95
☐	27260	**WILD SWAN** Celeste De Blasis	$5.95
☐	25692	**SWAN'S CHANCE** Celeste De Blasis	$5.95
☐	27790	**A WOMAN OF SUBSTANCE** Barbara Taylor Bradford	$5.95

Audio

☐ **SEPTEMBER** by Rosamunde Pilcher Performance by Lynn Redgrave 180 Mins. Double Cassette	45241-X	$15.95
☐ **THE SHELL SEEKERS** by Rosamunde Pilcher Performance by Lynn Redgrave 180 Mins. Double Cassette	48183-9	$14.95
☐ **COLD SASSY TREE** by Olive Ann Burns Performance by Richard Thomas 180 Mins. Double Cassette	45166-9	$14.95
☐ **NOBODY'S FAULT** by Nancy Holmes Performance by Geraldine James 180 Mins. Double Cassette	45250-9	$14.95